The Landscape of Loneliness

Brigita Orel

LEAF BY LEAF

Published by Leaf by Leaf
an imprint of Cinnamon Press,
Office 49019, PO Box 15113, Birmingham B2 2NJ
www.cinnamonpress.com
The right of Brigita Orel to be identified as author of this work has been asserted by her in accordance with the Copyright, Designs and Patent Act, 1988. © 2024 Brigita Orel.
Print Edition ISBN 978-1-78864-974-2
British Library Cataloguing in Publication Data. A CIP record for this book can be obtained from the British Library.
All rights reserved. No part of this publication may be reproduced, stored in a retrieval system, or transmitted in any form or by any means, electronic, mechanical, photocopying, recording or otherwise without the prior written permission of the publishers. This book may not be lent, hired out, resold or otherwise disposed of by way of trade in any form of binding or cover other than that in which it is published, without the prior consent of the publishers.
Designed and typeset in Adobe Caslon Pro by Cinnamon Press.
Cover design by Adam Craig © Adam Craig from original artwork by Jessica Bell.
Cinnamon Press is represented by Inpress.

About the Author

Brigita Orel has published short stories, essays, academic papers, and poems in numerous journals and anthologies. She studied creative writing at Swansea University in Wales. Her work was nominated for the Pushcart Prize and long and shortlisted for a number of other awards. She also writes for children and her picture book *The Pirate Tree* was published in 2019 by Lantana Publishing. She lives in Slovenia where she works as literary translator.

You can visit Brigita on her website—https://www.brigitaorel.com

or Instagram—https://www.instagram.com/brizitka/

For my parents and grandparents

The Landscape of Loneliness

ONE

Home. *Dom.* I try pronouncing it in my mother tongue but it sounds sharp-edged and unpractised. The blue-rinse lady across the aisle frowns at me. Her disapproval reminds me of the good old Slovenia I left behind almost a decade ago.

Everything about the landscape through the grimy bus window is familiar, yet alien. A home that hasn't felt like home for years.

My stomach roils and my clammy hand slips on the bar by the door when I step down onto the pavement, legs wobbly from the long ride.

The driver hauls my suitcase from the bus's underbelly. I drag it from the kerb and sit on it. Every breath threatens to bring up more than air. I massage my temples trying to alleviate the pounding headache caused by a long journey, dread, and a lack of food.

The movement of people at the bus terminal makes me dizzy, so I close my eyes for a second to shut it all out. The smell of the place awakens feelings in me that have lain dormant for years. I can't believe I'm back. I haven't forgotten how much I hated this place. I can't decide now whether I still do.

I pick up my laptop bag and struggle to drag the suitcase across the square's uneven paving stones. Once I leave the last of the houses behind, I feel relieved. I realise I'm terrified of running into someone I know and having to explain why I'm here, or worse, why I left.

I pant as I walk up the slight incline to the top of the hill that separates the house from the village. I should have packed less. I'm going to stay a couple of weeks at most. As soon as my father's health stabilises, I'll go back to Melbourne. Last year, the warmer weather brought large crowds to dine al fresco. I will be needed in the kitchen by the beginning of September at the latest.

In the valley below, the white-plastered house of my childhood sits under the tall linden tree. Across the road from it is Mrs Vidic's house, only hers is in the shade of a chestnut tree with half of its branches withered. Its roof looks new. The bridge that spans the river three hundred metres up from the two houses seems to have been renovated too. Floods often damaged it, with tree trunks and other debris catching behind the central support until the steel frame showed under the concrete.

I walk the last part of the way faster as it is all downhill. Before I can prepare myself, I'm standing in front of our house. I let my breath out and try the door handle. I don't remember ever finding that door locked, day or night, so it shocks me when it doesn't open.

Ivy covers the left side of the house, and the shutters on the second floor don't seem to open any more. Weeds sprout between the flagstones under my feet, and a plastic bag caught in the trellis above flutters in the breeze.

I brush off dirt crusted on the key from days of lying in the rosemary pot by the door. The paint around the door handle is peeling and as I push the door open, I notice that the milky pane of glass is cracked in the bottom left corner.

The hallway smells musty and there is another smell thick in the air, too. Cabbage, I think. My father has never been much of a cook. He probably lived off cabbage and potatoes.

The past meanders through the house, showing me around, pointing out things I have forgotten, like the yellowing postcards from the Yugoslav Riviera on the doors of the kitchen cupboard; or the grandfather clock with chains and weights that look like cones. As a child, I thought my father had gathered the cones in the woods and tied them to the clock to make it more fun.

An open book lies on the kitchen table, half covering the circle of scorched wood in the middle. Next to it sit two X-ray scans, large format, murky like the bottom of the river that runs past the house. A stark reminder of why I am here.

I step into the living room and it's as dark as I remember it. I pull the heavy curtains open. The crucifix above the door is tilted to the side. If Grandpa were here, he would reach up and right it.

Out of nowhere, the first drops of rain patter on the tin roof of the woodshed. The soft rain turns into a downpour, and within minutes, the garden fills with frothing water. The white sheet of rain mesmerises me. Yves used to say me liking rain proved I was impractical and given to daydreaming. I suspect he might be right.

The rain stops as abruptly as it started. A rivulet tinkles down the drainpipe. The shower has washed away some of the debris from the tarp covering my father's car. From the amount of leaves and twigs on it, it's clear he hasn't used it in ages. I wonder if it will still start.

My reflection in the windowpane stares back at me in all its blurry paleness. If only I could call Yves to tell him about the last few days, all the worrying about my father and about coming home, how unwell I've been for weeks, ever since he left, in fact, about how I miss him so much I feel hollow inside.

But it's Miren I ring.

"You've arrived already?" she says. After thirty-six hours on the move, I'd say finally rather than already. "How are you feeling?" she adds without waiting for my response.

"Odd. I feel odd being here after all this time." I don't have anything of note to tell her but I need to speak to someone to avoid the echoing silence in the house. Following the noise of rush hour at the bistro, the bustling airport, the crowded bus, this change is too sudden. I hear a bird out in the garden and the murmuring river further away, but the sounds are softer, diverse, and unfamiliar, unlike the uniform city noise.

"You'll be fine. You'll slip right back into things, you'll see," she says.

Will I? And how will that make it any easier?

"How's things back… in Melbourne?" I want to say "back home", but the familiar feel of the kitchen worktop I'm leaning against reminds me of where I am. This kitchen is part of me but at the same time it raises the question of who I am.

"Don't worry about us. Everything's in order here. Take care of your dad, and then hurry back, eh?" There is a smile in Miren's voice. I can imagine her rushing around preparing everything before they open for dinner while she holds the phone between her cheek and shoulder. I couldn't have asked for a better sous-chef; she's efficient and able to multitask. More importantly, she's become a good friend.

"I don't know yet how long I'll be gone," I say. Part of me hopes she will say they need me back promptly. Part of me feels the need to stay long enough for all this to become familiar again.

"Jeff says hi and take care," Miren says. "Oh, and there's something else. Someone was here looking for you. An old man."

"Walt?" The name bursts out of me and my lips stretch in a smile. I don't have a habit of connecting with strangers when first meeting them, but Walt was different. He reminded me of my father but also of how lost I sometimes felt, displaced, just like him after he relocated to Melbourne.

"Yes, that's him. Said you promised to cook for him. He looked upset when Jeff told him you weren't here. But he loved the food."

I feel terrible for not being there when he finally came. "Did he say anything?"

"You mean did he leave a message for you? Not that I know of. Sorry." Miren sounds confused, unable to comprehend who the old man is to me.

"Thanks for telling me," I say. "I'll explain when I get back. Keep me posted, please."

"Of course, Chef. And Nina..." For a moment, all I hear are the clanging of pots, people talking, and the coffee machine frothing milk. The kitchen staff are ready for the coffee break just before service starts. I miss it already. I'd give anything to be there with the people I love instead of in this quiet tomb. "Everything happens for a reason," Miren says, dispelling my thoughts. "Keep an open mind and don't be stubborn," she finishes.

I chuckle self-consciously. "I'm not stubborn."

"You are when you ignore the things you don't like," Miren says.

I want to argue but that would only prove her point.

The next morning, at the hospital, I open the door to my father's room and recoil at the smell of illness and old age.

"*Dobro jutro*," I say quietly, reluctant to disturb the patients.

One of them snores lightly, but the one in the bed by the window is sat reading and he looks up at me over the rim of his glasses. He nods in response.

My father's eyes are open but he doesn't react to my presence. My heart races when I think maybe he has died. Then his chest heaves in a halting breath. I've never seen anyone breathe with such obvious difficulty; it looks more like the pushing and pulling of a burden. I inhale deeply, as if to help him.

The man by the window stirs again. He gestures to the slightly open window. "Draught," he says.

"*Oprostite*," I say, and hurry to close the door.

My father lifts his head from the pillow at the noise, blinking, his white hair plastered to his forehead.

"Hello, *tata*. It's me, Nina."

I can't make myself sit on the bed. What if I dislodge the drips and catheters? He looks fragile. Trying to hug him as he's lying down would just be awkward. I don't remember when we last hugged. I'm so unprepared for how sad that makes me feel I wrap my arms around my middle, and I don't know if it's to make up for the lack of hugs or to keep myself from falling to pieces. After my long absence, being here feels wrong. As if I don't have a right to it. But also, our first meeting in three years should happen in happier circumstances. Only, there never have been happier circumstances with us. Except perhaps when I was very little, beyond the reach of my memory.

"Nina?" He struggles to sit up.

I bend, placing my hand on his bony shoulder. "Yes, it's me, *tata*. Don't strain yourself."

I borrow the chair by the sleeping man's bed and tiptoe back, sitting between the beds with my back to the man with the newspaper. I wish we had more privacy.

"I couldn't come earlier. I'm sorry." I can't admit to him that the return home unsettled me so much I needed the whole afternoon after I arrived to compose myself.

My father's grimace turns into a smile and his eyes fill with tears. I pat his hand, embarrassed by how overemotional he's become since I last saw him. His fingers twitch but he doesn't have the strength for anything more.

I wonder about my health because of the disquieting pattern my father's tumour and my mother's breast cancer have established. I wonder, too, if there's any truth in Miren's claims that unhappiness is more likely to cause cancer than smoking and fried food.

"I'm glad you came." He licks his dry lips. "These two don't talk much." A smile lights up his eyes even as he struggles with words. "I was bored."

I try smiling but it's harder than I remember. "How are you feeling?"

"Not myself."

"Are you in pain?" I whisper. I have to force myself to

ask the intimate question.

"Not much."

His silhouette under the sheet is so flimsy. Is there enough of him left to experience pain at all?

"Why didn't you tell me? Why didn't you go to the doctor's earlier?" I can't stop myself although guilt is the last thing he needs. But sitting at his bedside, I feel guilty, too; guilty because I'm angry with him for not telling me sooner; because I found leaving Melbourne inconvenient; because I blame him for all the uneasy feelings that have simmered in me since I stepped back into my childhood home the day before.

I didn't have time to say goodbye to my mother because she told me about her cancer too late. My then boyfriend and I were changing flights in Hamburg on our way back from a holiday when my father called to tell me. I left my boyfriend to return to Stockholm alone and flew home. I was still too late.

"You couldn't have done anything," my father now says.

The simple truth of his words shakes me. He is my father; I should be able to help him. But have I ever even tried?

He waves his hand vaguely as if to say "it doesn't matter". "How... how have you been?"

Several possible answers flash through my mind, each accompanied by a different unease. Telling him I've started to feel at home in Australia seems traitorous. Lying to him on his sickbed is equally disturbing. I settle for, "Good. I like Melbourne."

"Job?" He swallows with difficulty, his Adam's apple bobbing sharply under the stubbled grey skin.

"I'm a chef at a lovely bistro. You'd like it. Good food."

"Just like Nelida." He licks his cracked lips. "She loved cooking." He gulps. "She died."

Does he think I've forgotten that my mother died? Or is he reminding himself?

He winces and starts coughing.

I jump up to help him but then I just stand there. I don't know what to do. He tries speaking between coughs. At last, I understand he wants water. I hold the glass to his mouth and he sips as I imagine a bird would—barely a drop.

"Better?" I ask. A moment passes before I realise I spoke in English. "*Bolje?*"

He settles. For the first few breaths, his chest rumbles like distant thunder.

The silence is awkward but I can't find anything to say. I look everywhere but at him—the sagging door of the wardrobe with a pair of shoes with the soles worn out unevenly on the bottom shelf, the plaster in the corner by the door that's coming off, the scarred and torn linoleum.

My father's eyes close and I think he must have fallen asleep. But then his eyes pop open, his gaze lost and scared. "Nelida?"

"No, Father, it's me, Nina. Mother's gone," I whisper, ashamed the other patient might witness my father's confusion, which even my words don't seem to clear. "You're tired, Father. I'll go now and come back tomorrow." At the thought of the long, winding road home my stomach churns. "Have a rest." I pat his shoulder and wonder how much his afflicted brain still lets him feel things. "I'll come back."

TWO

I wake in the disorienting darkness and for a moment I think I'm in my flat in Middle Park. Then the apple tree outside the window rustles, the grandfather clock chimes a quarter past some ungodly hour, and the contours of my childhood home emerge from the dimness. I turn over and try to go back to sleep but it's futile.

I walk down the hallway without turning the light on. I run into the sharp edge of a wardrobe. My memory of the place isn't as good as I thought.

The yellowish tungsten light turns the kitchen into a ghost of the past. The cupboards shine with grease. The appliances are off-white with age and use; the extractor hood is covered in dust. A large spiderweb spreads between the hood and the wall as if to hold the two together.

My memory of the kitchen and its current state match down to the threadbare curtains and the chipped glass light fixture, but what was once the most comfortable room in the house now seems inadequate and poor.

Once I finish cleaning the kitchen, the pale early morning illuminates the room but does little to brighten it.

I browse the shelf next to the fridge and pull out my mother's favourite cookbook. Its edges are worn with love, filled with her even writing as she saved her own recipes between the pages, added notes to the existing ones, doodled in the margins while she waited for the sponge cake to bake, and jotted down dear moments and memories. It's a scrapbook of our family life, such as it was.

I browse through the cookbook, but I can't decide on any of the recipes. Instead, I open the fridge for inspiration. The solitary wedge of cheese, two eggs, and some ricotta look unappetising in the empty space. None are past their use-by date. My father must have bought them just before he was taken to hospital. I dig out a sack of potatoes from the cupboard under the sink. I remember as a child how we ate jacket potatoes with cottage cheese, so I wash them, and boil them in their jackets.

After a time I use a toothpick, like my mother taught me, to check if the potatoes are cooked. I reach to grab the oven glove but then hesitate. Its red-dotted fabric reminds me of the day I first saw the pattern.

I had spent that summer afternoon in the garden, helping my father dig up a dead apple tree. While he put the tools away in the shed, I poked the burning heap of dry branches. I liked that by digging up the tree carcass we had made space for a currant bush. My mother made delicious blackcurrant cordial.

Through the crackling of the last of the flames, my mother's voice reached me around the corner of the house. I was starving from all the digging, dragging, and sawing, so my first thought was her calling us in to dinner. I ran towards the house and smiled when I heard Auntie Marija. She'd gone away the week before and no one would tell me where, or when she'd be back.

I hesitated as the voices rose. I waited at the corner, deciding whether to move forwards or quietly go back, and if staying meant I was eavesdropping.

Before I made a move one way or the other, Mum said, "And where is she supposed to wear this dress to? The garden?"

Who? What dress? I wondered.

"I thought maybe for her birthday," Auntie Marija said. She sounded as unsure and small as me when Mum frowned at me.

"She'll have outgrown it by then. Besides, a sleeveless dress in winter?"

"She'll celebrate indoors, won't she?"

I moved forwards enough to see Auntie Marija, who stood up straight, but Mum was half a head taller still. A red dress with black polka dots hung from Mum's hand. It looked wonderful. I didn't understand why Mum was so upset.

"In any case, it's crazy to buy a dress she'll wear once, if at all."

Her back turned to me, I couldn't see Mum's expression, but I heard the sharpness in her voice. She stood really straight. It was strange seeing her raise her voice at a grown-up. Stranger still that it was my quiet, kind aunt.

"Well, it was my choice to buy it," Auntie Marija said. "I wanted Nina to have something nice from me."

Auntie Marija disappeared into the house without waiting for Mum's answer. I drew back, afraid Mum would catch me spying now that she was no longer busy.

I decided it would be best to pretend I hadn't heard a thing. I was certain things would return to normal by dinner time, and Auntie Marija would be allowed to give me the dress.

But there was no gift waiting for me at the dinner table. Auntie Marija was sitting in her usual spot in the corner. Grandpa was mumbling something under his breath, his bushy eyebrows lowered.

Dad was the last to come in, wiping his washed hands on his jeans, which were so dirty because of this habit of his that they probably stained his hands all over again. He looked around the room, frowned, and sat at his end of the table. He made a lot of noise with his spoon and the bread knife, coughing as if coming down with a cold in the middle of the summer. I could tell he was doing it all on purpose.

Mum put the pot with the vegetable soup on the table with a bang. I opened my mouth to tell her she'd forgotten the pot stand, but something in her face stopped me. The smell of the scorching wood of the table made me want to sneeze.

"Did you have a good trip?" I asked Auntie Marija.

She looked at me, startled. Grandpa muttered.

"Where did you go? Did you buy anything?"

Her lips started to move, but then she pressed them together again.

"Eat," Mum said.

Dad stopped making so much noise and ate. He didn't even scrape the spoon against the bottom of the bowl as he usually did.

Grandpa slurped the soup, piercing me with his grey eyes, and Auntie Marija gripped her clean spoon in her hand, her eyes red and popping out of her head.

I bent my head and ate the soup as my tears dripped

into the bowl. I didn't understand why everyone seemed angry with me.

Most of the time in my childhood, I felt I couldn't do anything right. As if, just by being me, I was somehow in the wrong.

It surprises me how much, thinking back, the memory still hurts. Shaken, I clumsily peel the potatoes, slice them, and toss them into a bowl to cool. I mash the ricotta with a fork and add yoghurt. Then chives, parsley, salt, and pepper. When the potatoes stop steaming, I stir in the ricotta.

I'm impatient to taste the dish after twenty years. But it isn't as expected. There are no flashbacks to be found in the fresh ricotta, no memories in the creaminess of the potatoes. Even the chives are a let-down as I used the dried ones I found in the cupboard.

All the disappointing squashy potatoes remind me of is a family torn apart by some mysterious force I don't comprehend even as an adult. They remind me of a relationship with a man that I have ended twice even though I still love him. Of my father in hospital and my mother buried and no member of the family left but me. I cry for all of it, in the middle of the kitchen where I spent the first half of my life and that I hated the other half.

I wipe my face with a kitchen towel when the tears stop. The grandfather clock chimes eight in the morning, and I'm already tired from being awake for hours. The birds outside have fallen silent one by one, their morning song finished. I reach again for my mother's cookbook. For years after I left, I never thought of it. It was only after I'd promised Walt I'd cook him a Slovenian dish that I remembered my mother's recipes and how she'd filled the margins of her cookbook with her recommendations and the changes she'd made to the recipes. It's strange how reluctant I am now to let go of something I haven't thought about for so long.

My fingers linger on the torn protective jacket at the back. I wonder if my mother felt the same way about this book as I do now. Did it feel like our family's bible to her? Or was it just an old cookbook, the edges smudged and pages creased, its jacket torn and taped together? She'd probably laugh at me for being so amazed by a book of recipes she knew by heart anyway.

Heavy and drowsy from jet lag and the frenzied cleaning earlier, I return barefoot to the couch in the guest room at the back of the house. The ache in the small of my back reminds me of how uncomfortable the sagging couch is. I wonder when the physical ache will become unpleasant enough for me to face the stifling memories and venture to the bedrooms on the first floor. But until I gather the courage, the couch will do.

I find momentary relief in the cool sheets, but soon I'm perspiring with an anxiety I can't place. My stomach roils and the little food I ate ends up in the toilet. When I flush, I wonder when I last managed to keep a meal down. It must have been before my departure from Melbourne. I didn't expect the return home to be so stressful.

My father's cough echoes halfway down the hospital hallway. I always used to worry my father would get lung cancer because he'd been smoking for fifty years. I didn't expect a liver tumour.

I open the door slowly, more out of fear of what I might find than consideration for the frail patients.

My father's face is flushed and he's still gasping after the rattling cough. It is only a little over twelve hours since I saw him, but he looks weaker. I try to find consolation in the doctor's explanation that it is the quick type of growth and so the pain will be over soon. But panic finds me instead. Guilt gnaws at me because my father and I have become strangers since my mother's death. I can't believe, in the last year, I only called him twice. But we have nothing to say to each other. We used to talk. My earliest memories of him are pleasant; laughter echoes in my mind as I think of those first years of my life. I've no idea where along the way we lost all that. Or why.

My father doesn't react as I sit in the chair by his bed. Has he recognised me at all? His left hand fidgets with the hem of the blanket.

"Hello. *Tata?*"

His eyes flit to me but go blurry the next second. His morphine dose must have been increased.

I try a second time. "*Tata?*"

His head jerks and his eyes settle on me, this time for longer. "Nina."

I breathe a sigh of relief. It's a lonely feeling, not being recognised by one's own parent. Was that how he felt when I didn't call for long periods? When I only told him I had moved to Melbourne a week after the fact? When I mistakenly spoke in English instead of his mother tongue?

"How was your night?"

He opens his mouth but all that comes out is a feeble croak. He nods instead.

"Do you need anything?" I'm desperate to fill the silence, to hide how I feel like an impostor with no right to be here. I haven't been a daughter for years. I've been too preoccupied with my own life to spare him a thought.

But I remember the tension and the strange silences between my parents when I was a child. How I always felt an outsider. The feeling of being unwanted drove me away. If I hadn't had a reason, perhaps I wouldn't have left. His health might have been better if I had cooked for him; we might have been living close to one another; maybe I would have had a family and he would have taught his grandchildren fishing.

But thinking about the what ifs makes us hungry for the things we cannot have. I learned that the first time Yves and I ended our relationship.

I left, and that's that.

"You came back," my father says. As he exhales the words, even his breath is sturdier than his body. I blink away my tears, feeling foolish for being emotional now when it's too late.

"Remember how you used to send me to the shop for ice cream when I was little? We ate so much ice cream every summer." The memory comes to me unbidden and the longing it brings is sharp.

He would give me a few coins and send me to the shop over a kilometre away. I would run the last part of the way back, from where I could see the river bend and the two solitary houses on its bank, down the dusty road, all the way to the tall linden tree that offered a bit of shade during the worst of the afternoon heat. The tree seemed so tall to me I used to think one day I would look up and see a cloud snagged on it.

"I loved ice cream." He gulps.

"Me, too."

Sun lights up the room as if to check if there is still someone in there worth warming. Its brightness deepens the lines on my father's face. It makes him seem transparent, the way one's eyelids feel when staring at the sun through closed eyes. I half expect to see the pillow through his face. His eyes drift shut.

I lean back in my chair to wait for him to wake again.

The newspaper reader from my last visit lies on his back, staring through the window. "When he goes like that"—the man's voice cuts through my thoughts— "it's sometimes hours before he wakes again." He turns his head, his watery hazel eyes staring at me, unblinking, as if waiting to see how I'll react. "Just so you know if you intend to wait it out."

I don't know if he is being helpful or trying to get me to go. I want to stay, but if he is right, what good will it do me to waste my time waiting? I decide to leave.

The end of July heat swamps me as I hurry out through the glass entrance. The seat of the car is hot and the air stuffy, stinking of overheated plastic. My father's old Renault 5 has been so neglected it's a struggle to start it every time. It doesn't have air conditioning, but even with the scorching interior, it's a relief to be out of the hospital.

The flagstones in front of the house are dappled with sun spots through the vine trellis. I've been resting on the bench underneath for half an hour but my stomach still hasn't settled after the winding drive home. I need a better car. The Renault 5 is fine for the short drive into the village, but for the thirty-minute trip to the hospital it's as comfortable as a mousetrap.

Heat wafts from the nearby asphalt road. The smell reminds me of burnt caramel. The leaves of the linden tree flicker from the heat rather than the breeze. The stretch of grass between our house and Mrs Vidic's is parched.

In the half hour I have been sitting here, not a single car has passed. I'm surprised to find it pleasant, this silence, but after a while it's almost like it becomes too loud, making my mind buzz.

I enter the cool house and the outside warmth clings to me like an extra layer of clothes. I follow my instincts more than relying on my eyes because the house is thrust into darkness, daylight forming patterns in places where it seeps in through the slats of the shutters. It's quiet and dreamy, with the dark furniture, its edges round with wear and history, and the heavy curtains I used to find suffocating.

My stomach grumbles with hunger. I walk into the pantry by the kitchen. The room is narrow, with shelves covering the two longer walls. Now half empty, it looks twice as big as when it was stocked with preserves and food. I miss the smells from my childhood: crab apples, pancetta, and dried pear slices. Dust and dead spiders cover most shelves now. Childhood homes shouldn't smell like mould.

The labels on the few remaining glass jars are chewed to pieces and transformed into mouse droppings. I can tell there's pear compote in one jar and cherry jam in another. I say the Slovenian words aloud, practising them. I know most gastronomic terms in French and English but almost none in Slovenian. The trouble I've had with even the most common Slovenian expressions this past week makes me realise eight years abroad is a long time.

In the large freezer, I find two steaks, which look brown and unappetising, and five packets of plums marked with last year's date. I throw the steaks away and take one packet of plums to the kitchen.

Perhaps making something to remind me of the best times I spent with my mother will console my stomach enough to keep the food down.

I remember one day my mother made dumplings for dinner. She called them "*knedlji*", and I had no idea then how similar that word was to the English "kneading", which I learned much later, probably in cookery school in Stockholm or Paris.

I wash potatoes and toss them in a pot to boil, all the while remembering how strange my mother's relationship with her sister was, not at all how I had imagined sisters behaved. There was a sort of ruthlessness in my mother I hadn't noticed before that day.

I can't remember where my father was that evening but I imagine he was at the pub. Marija entered the kitchen just as my mother and I sat at the table to eat. My aunt's face looked pale through the steam coming off my plate of plum dumplings. The tablecloth was white, with a purple border, and I thought how it suited our meal, a purple delight. I spooned sugar on my dumplings and Marija sighed, "Oh, *knedlji*."

"There are none left," my mother said without looking up from her plate.

I felt sorry for my aunt, but I didn't dare intervene on her behalf for fear of losing the privilege of having my own dumplings.

My aunt perched on the edge of her chair, watching us

eat. But my mother's silence stretched long past dinner. I tried to fill the quiet with silly rambling, which my mother ignored and Marija tolerated with a wan smile.

I was reading in bed later when my mother knocked on my door. She stopped in the doorway and smiled. "Goodnight now."

"I'll just finish this," I said, showing her the picture book I had propped on my knees.

My mother's fidgety fingers dropped the kitchen towel she held. She picked it up and said, "*Knedlji* are our special treat, no?"

Unsure what she was asking, I nodded. This was about Marija, I understood that much, but I didn't know exactly what about her and what it had to do with dumplings.

"She can't take that away from me," my mother added, more to herself than to me. I barely heard the door closing, she disappeared from my room so quietly.

I wish the fog of memories would vanish like that, too—disperse like the steam from the potatoes as I strain them. But snippets from the past cloud my thoughts. I try to ignore them, but there is no stopping the memories.

THREE

The music reminded me of the tune in my spinning ballerina music box. I saw the bright lights all the way from the car park. The noise got louder and louder with each step nearer the fairground. I pressed my hands over my ears but it didn't make much difference.

"Look at that Ferris wheel," Mum said, and she sounded as amazed as I felt. "It's enormous."

I imagined that if I found myself in the top pod and stood on tiptoes and stretched my arms, I could almost touch the shiny fat moon above. The longer I stared up at the wheel, the smaller I felt. I lowered my eyes to Mum and Dad on either side of me.

"Can I go?" I asked, half-hopeful, half-scared they would say yes.

Mum gave me a look. "You can go on the cups with me," she said.

That was better than nothing. I would ask for candy floss later, after the cups. It had got in my hair when I ate it on the cups last time we were here. I didn't remember the big wheel. Just the cups with Mum and two pigs Dad and I had ridden on the merry-go-round. It was always just two rides, one with Mum and one with Dad. We couldn't afford more, Dad had said.

"You promised the bumper cars, too," I said to Dad. He

didn't look at me. "Dad?"

"Kids are strapped in," he said to Mum when she raised her eyebrows.

I could tell she didn't agree with me going on the bumper cars. Dad wasn't convinced either. But I had time; we had only just got here.

I floated like a balloon as Mum pulled me behind her through the crowds. The lights made the fair magical, but my ears hurt from all the noise. Even when I could distinguish individual words amidst the cries and laughter, they didn't make sense to me. Dad said they spoke a different language because we were in Italy. It wasn't a long way from home but it was all so strange. The houses looked different and there was an unfamiliar smell. But I liked the fair rides.

I was excited when Dad went to buy a token for one bumper car ride. He counted the coins carefully. They were called lira. My hand felt squished and clammy in Mum's grip as we waited for Dad to return.

In all the excitement, I tripped over my feet when the cars stopped, and Dad led me towards them.

"Which one?" he asked.

There were marvellous red ones, and blue, and there was one shiny silver car in the corner furthest from us.

"Pick one, come on."

Everyone else was seated and ready for the ride. There were too many cars there. I looked at a yellow one, then back to the red, green and orange, silver, blue… I shuffled my feet and jumped on the spot a little, but the choice was too hard.

"The si—" I didn't manage to finish; Dad was already pulling me to the nearest empty bumper car.

"But Dad—" I had wanted the silver one.

"We'll miss the ride, Nina."

I fought him as he buckled me in, but then there was a loud sound and the other cars moved. I gave in, slumping against the seat. The next second someone bumped into us from behind and I was thrown forwards, catching myself against the dashboard.

"Hold on!" Dad yelled, his eyes sparkling.

I grinned as the air whooshed by when a red bumper car jetted past us.

Sparks flew from the meshed ceiling, and the music was louder than ever. The cars kept hitting us from all directions. Dad tried to steer clear of them and find a path in between, but there were always some cars in the way. If only there was enough space in the car for Mum to come along for the ride.

The car drew to a stop and I thought it had broken down, but when I looked around all the other cars were still, too.

"Off we go," Dad said.

"It's not over yet, is it?" We'd only just started. "Can we go again?"

Dad unbuckled the seat belt, grinning. "It was enough, love. Next time."

He seemed to have enjoyed the ride. Maybe I could convince him. "Dad..." But he guided me towards where Mum waited for us. "Just one more," I begged.

Mum took hold of my hand and Dad dropped back and walked behind us as we weaved through the people.

"Did you have fun?" Mum asked. "Let's go on the cups."

If I protested too much, I might not get the candy floss,

so I followed Mum and climbed into the nearest cup.

We waited for the cups to fill, and I searched for Dad in the crowd at the edge of the cups ride. I couldn't find him. I was sad that he wouldn't see us spin around and laugh until our stomachs hurt.

There were two girls in the cup next to ours. They looked exactly the same down to the last button on their floral dresses.

"Twins," Mum said before I could ask.

"What's that?"

"Sisters who were born together and are identical."

"Like you and Auntie Marija?" I asked.

"No, not like me and Auntie Marija."

I wasn't sure whether that meant they weren't twins or they weren't alike.

An entire family crammed themselves into the cup on our other side. I worried how they would all fit since Dad had always said there wasn't enough space in the cup for him to join us.

The bell sounded and we moved, ever more quickly. I looked up. The twinkling lights in the canopy were magical. I wished Dad were with us to see it. I wished the fair rides would never end.

Mum and I joined Dad in the crowd. Dizzy from the rides and exhausted now the thrill of the fair was over, I dragged my feet on the way to the car. Dad buckled me in and the next second my head felt too heavy for me to hold up.

I was jostled around and Dad was saying something but I didn't know what was going on. Even as I strained to open my eyes, darkness remained.

Car doors slammed, and a bright light turned on in the

distance. I recognised our front door underneath it. Dad's face smiled above me as he carried me to the house.

"You fell asleep in the car," he said. He sounded far away.

"I just want one more ride." The words were like chewing gum in my mouth, sticking to my teeth and tongue as I struggled to get them out.

"Next time."

Mum's chuckle behind us was warm and comforting like my favourite blanket.

The front door opened and there stood Auntie Marija. "Hello," she said, her hand pressed to her chest.

My eyes drifted shut and I yawned like the lion that appears before every *Tom and Jerry* cartoon. Dad still held me in his arms, but he didn't move. For a second, I thought I had fallen asleep as no one had spoken for so long, but just as I opened my eyes, Auntie Marija said, "I thought I'd hold dinner until you returned."

Dad didn't say anything and the distance between us and Mum and Auntie Marija grew as he carried me up the stairs and into my room. Mum and Auntie's voices followed us into the house and stopped somewhere downstairs. Muffled, they crept up the stairs like the fog that rose from the river on wet days. I didn't understand a word of what they were saying.

"Goodnight," Dad said.

"Night, Dad."

He closed the door as I lay in bed, still in my dress and socks. Dad's footsteps returned to the landing, but the voices below became louder and angrier, and suddenly Dad's steps went past my door again, down the hallway, and into my parents' bedroom.

Were they fighting over something? I strained to hear more, but the sounds seemed further and further away.

I woke to brilliant sunshine, with specks of light dancing on my blanket. Something obstructed the movement of my legs, and I pulled the covers off to free them.

The surprise only lasted a moment when I remembered we'd been at the fair the day before. The exciting memory of the bumper car ride and the crazy cups awakened me in a flash. The smell of stale popcorn and candy floss came from my hair and the pillow. We had arrived home so late Dad hadn't bothered changing me into pyjamas and I'd gone to bed in the dress I had worn to the fair. Now it was crumpled like Grandpa's handkerchiefs and tangled in my legs.

Grandpa was waiting for me in the kitchen.

"Where's Mum?" I asked.

"Good morning to you, too." His voice was grumbly, but his smile teasing. "She's gone to work."

Dad went to work early, but Mum only worked for a few hours every day, so she prepared breakfast for me before she left. Her being gone meant I had got up late. The rides at the fair had exhausted me. I barely remembered Dad carrying me to my room the night before. I remembered how Auntie Marija had appeared at the door. How Dad changed his mind and didn't go back downstairs after he had put me to bed.

I slid onto a chair at the table. Buttering a slice of bread, I asked, "Did Mum and Auntie Marija have a row last night?"

Grandpa's eyebrows rose high on his forehead. "Of course not," he said after a moment. Grandpa sometimes said things which weren't exactly true, but he always stuck by his words, so there was no point in trying to get anything more out of him.

I swatted away fruit flies dancing around the pears in the bowl on the table. When I turned one of the pears around, juice oozed out of a rotten patch, and more fruit flies stirred. I dropped the pear back into the bowl.

"Bugger!" Grandpa said.

I looked up. "What's wrong?"

"The milk has gone bad," Grandpa grumbled, and poured it into the sink.

I sighed and spread a lot of jam on the bread.

"Isn't that a bit too much, missy?"

"I took too much out of the jar. I can't put it back, can I, now that the butter's mixed in?" I wouldn't be so quick to say that to Mum but I knew Grandpa wouldn't be too cross. I'd seen him spread just as much jam on his bread. Although, I guess, he made up for it as he often ate it without butter or jam at all, just dunked it in warm milk.

He placed my Little Red Riding Hood pot in front of me. I peered at the drink. It looked like cocoa, but when I took a tiny sip, it tasted odd.

"I made it with water," he said.

It didn't go down as easily, but I'd already pushed my luck with the jam. "Why does milk go bad?" I asked.

Grandpa thought. "That's the nature of things, I suppose; they spoil."

I stuffed the last piece of bread into my mouth and then struggled to talk. Mum would have had something to say about that, too. "But when the milk goes off, it doesn't really go bad, does it? You can drink sour milk, too."

Grandpa grinned. "There you have it. There's something good in bad things, too, eh?"

When I had finished eating and carried the pot to the sink, he wiped the table with the kitchen towel, leaving it crumpled on the worktop. He left the kitchen and I straightened the towel and folded it the way Mum liked to do.

On my way past the table, I remembered the spoiled fruit. I took it out to the compost heap.

Grandpa went to chop firewood next to the shed, while I planted apple seeds in the garden and watered them. Our lunch was the leftover stew from the day before. Mum always made extra because Grandpa said he couldn't be bothered to cook at his age.

I could almost pretend I was alone at the table because after Auntie Marija had joined us, we all fell silent. I opened my mouth to ask her about the previous night, but Grandpa looked at me sternly as if he knew what I was thinking.

Sometimes it was difficult to tell why the grown-ups wanted me to do certain things. Especially when they communicated with frowns and looks. But sometimes even words were confusing. A while before, Dad had mixed up the dates and got a day off work the day after Mum had planned a trip to the zoo, so we couldn't go and I cried.

"Why can't we go?" I asked. I'd been so looking forward to it. I sniffled and wiped my face on my sleeve.

"Ask your father," Mum said, her face dark.

Dad's lips moved but no words came out. He hung his head.

"Well done," Mum said to Dad, and left the kitchen.

I didn't understand. Hadn't she just said Dad had messed up?

"It's all your fault," I spat, although I didn't know why and what was his fault. I had stomped out and kicked Dad's shoes in the hallway, too.

Whenever I wasn't sure what grown-ups were telling me, I got this feeling in my stomach that something awful would happen if I didn't get it right. Usually, it was easier to talk with Grandpa than with Mum or Dad, but not this time. I waited for Grandpa to say something, but he just ate the stew, staring at his bowl.

After lunch, Auntie Marija waved for me to follow her. We climbed up to her attic room in silence. I jumped a little as I sat on her bed, loving how wobbly the soft mattress was.

Auntie Marija went to her wardrobe. The door squealed as she opened it. "You're such a good girl," she said, her head hidden in her overalls and housecoats.

People didn't say such things to me—except for Grandpa once—so I didn't know what to say.

But it seemed like Auntie Marija didn't expect me to say anything, because the next moment, she brought a doll from her wardrobe and offered it to me. It was made of straw and it looked delicate but it felt surprisingly firm as I held it in my hand. Its face was painted on, but it had little straw arms and legs poking from under a pretty decorated skirt.

"Is this for me?" I asked, turning it in my hand, admiring the tiny straw hat on its head.

Auntie Marija nodded when I lifted my eyes to her, her face glowing as if she were the one getting a present. "But keep it in this room."

"Oh."

She must have seen my surprise because she said, "Your mum could get upset about me giving you a present when it's not your birthday."

I was disappointed I couldn't take it with me, but the doll was too pretty for me to stay sad for long. Auntie Marija lent me her prettiest handkerchief to use as a dress for the doll, and I played on her bed. Every time I looked up, Auntie Marija was watching me from the chair by the window, smiling. I smiled back. I liked that we shared a secret.

When Mum called my name from downstairs, it was like I had woken from a dream.

Auntie Marija jumped up, eyes wide. "I forgot about the time," she said, and rushed me out the door, but she didn't follow me down.

I found Mum in the kitchen. I watched her prepare dinner, standing on a stool next to her, and I soon forgot about Auntie Marija and the doll.

Sometimes, Mum let me help cook now that I could reach the tap and the top cabinets with the help of a stool. Two days before, I tried reaching a glass in the cupboard and the stool overturned. I bruised my elbow when I fell. Dad found me. He promised he wouldn't tell Mum I'd broken the glass. I kept my sleeves down to hide my bruise.

Mum looked over at me and smiled. "Hungry?"

I nodded. My mouth watered as I smelled the boiled potatoes, so delicious and warm, and the green herb Mum used in the cottage cheese.

The grandfather clock in the living room chimed. Right on time, Dad stamped his feet on the outside steps.

Despite the noises in the hallway, Mum didn't pause in mashing the cottage cheese until it was shiny.

"Evening," Dad said, entering the kitchen.

"Hi," I said, wanting to distract Mum from griping about Dad wiping his washed hands on his worn jeans. She always complained about it.

"Go set the table," Mum said to me.

That I could peel jacket potatoes on my own was the second unexpected present that day. I was allowed my own small knife, and took great care not to nick my fingers. I didn't want to lose the privilege of being treated like a grown-up. I blew on my fingers when the potatoes became too hot.

I'd asked Mum earlier why Grandpa and Auntie Marija weren't joining us, but she just mumbled. I hated it when the grown-ups mumbled.

Then Dad said, "She shouldn't be allowed a knife. She's only six."

Was he talking about me? I forgot about the potatoes for a moment, but I kept my eyes lowered so they wouldn't notice I was listening.

"She's skilful. And careful," Mum said.

"She's six."

It was best to keep quiet in these situations, but I couldn't stop myself from blurting out, "I won't cut myself."

They ignored me.

"Are you trying to tell me how to raise my daughter?" Mum said.

I glanced at Dad from the corner of my eye. His face was pinched, his lips moving silently as if he was trying to stop himself from saying something. I felt sorry for him because I imagined it must have hurt, those words pushing at his teeth to be let out, and him struggling to hold them back.

My eyes were glued onto Mum and Dad's faces. It was as though a chasm opened between them and I was teetering on its edge, about to drop into the hole. Neither of them moved as much as a centimetre, but the table between them seemed to grow bigger and the distance became as wide as our valley.

Dad placed his knife on the plate soundlessly, stood, and carried it to the sink. He walked just like Grandpa did in the mornings because of his aching joints.

I wondered what would happen with the potatoes he hadn't eaten. I wondered if I could have them.

Mum bent low over her meal.

The cold lumps of potato turned hard and dry in my mouth. Even the soft cottage cheese didn't moisten them. It was hard to swallow and one of the bits hurt me all the way down.

It was pitch-dark when something woke me later that night. Fear shot through me, but then I recognised Dad's footsteps as he moved down the hall.

There was silence for the next moment. I waited. Their voices rose and I wondered if they were still arguing about me using the knife. It was so silly. It was just a knife, after all. And I was really careful.

One afternoon, Mum brought a large basket of pea pods into the kitchen. I was drawing at the table, occasionally munching on the ends of my colouring pencils because I liked the taste of the coloured middle.

Mum set the basket on the chair across from me. She

brought a blue enamel bowl with white dots to the table and then shelled the peas. I loved watching her quick fingers as she worked. The peas dropped into the bowl, first with a loud noise, but the more peas there were in it, the softer the sound became.

"Can I try?" I asked.

I came round the table to sit next to her. Mum pushed the basket closer to me.

When Mum did it, it looked easy, but I struggled to open my first pod, and a piece of it got stuck under my nail. My colour-speckled fingers hurt from trying so hard when I did the second one. But then a pea leaped out of the pod like a tiny green frog, shot across the table, bounced off my notebook, and fell off the edge. Mum's fingers stopped moving. Her eyes followed the pea as it rolled to its hiding place in the dust under the chair in the corner.

She burst out laughing. I was so relieved when she didn't shout at me for playing with food.

That something so silly and simple could make Mum laugh spurred me on and I tried repeating it.

Mum pointed the pod in her hands towards me and when she pulled it open, a pea shot me in the chin hard. Mum never even wanted to crawl with me into my tent in the garden but she would do this?

I laughed so hard my sides hurt. I wanted her to shoot peas at me every day, all day long. I wished her face would always look so bright. I wished Dad or Auntie Marija would never walk through the door and make the kitchen fall silent again. But I felt bad when I thought of the story of *The Princess and the Pea*. Auntie Marija only ever read it to me when we were alone and she told me not to tell

Mum.

The pinging of the peas on the table and chairs died down. Mum's eyes were full of laughter and she wiped away her tears, stuffing the handkerchief in her sleeve. From time to time, she chuckled as she bent over the bowl where the mountain of peas had grown tall.

"Well, that was fun, you peashooter," she said, smiling at me.

I tried smiling back. Only when the two of us were alone in the kitchen did her face soften and her eyes fill with an expression that made my stomach feel strange. Because I knew, sooner or later, her face would harden again and the sharp look in her eyes would make me wonder what I had done wrong.

That summer, the swimming season started long before school ended. It was torture waiting for the holidays to begin, but once the end of June came around, it became clear that although my school friends and I had made a promise to spend the summer together, they were much too busy to find the time to play with me.

So I lay in the shade of the willow trees and bushes by the river alone, gathering colourful pieces of glass and perfect round stones. When it got too hot, I took a dip in the river.

My shaded spot was just warm enough today. Dad had gone in for a swim while I sat on a patch of grass, digging my toes into the gooey mix of sand and river mud. I loved it sliding against my feet, cooling them. The branches of the willow trees above moved in the breeze. The sunlight coming through the leaves was green and made my spot feel like fairyland and me a fairy princess. Over my shoulder, I could just see our house at the end of a narrow trail. I loved how the path zigzagged across the meadow and through the willows. Every time I came down to the river it was like going on a treasure hunt. The river was always different, the banks changed, the sand shifted, while the house and the hills and mountains behind it stayed the same.

I shrieked when Dad splashed me with water. I imagined the cold droplets sizzling on my hot skin the way milk sizzled on the range when it boiled over. Except river water smelled of moss and playing in the mud, while the burnt milk smell reminded me of Mum complaining about having to clean the mess.

Dad vanished into the bushes behind me. He returned a moment later, carrying a large coltsfoot leaf. With a small twig, he pinned the two edges together and offered the hat to me.

"To keep your head out of the sun," he said.

Mum sometimes made me flower wreaths, which I wore like a crown. Although this was no tiara, I put the elfish hat on my messy hair. Princesses had to behave while elves were allowed to be naughty, so perhaps being an elf rather than a fairy princess wasn't so bad.

We built a big castle in the sand, but the outer walls kept dissolving into shapeless mounds. There was more sand on my legs and arms than in our castle and I smelled like a swamp. Horseflies swarmed around me.

"We need to add a flag to our castle," Dad said, and went in search of something we could use.

I was finishing the last of the towers, which I had to support with twigs to keep the sand walls from crumpling.

All of a sudden, Mum spoke behind me. "There you are."

I turned to see her picking her way through the low trees towards me.

"Look, Mum, a castle. Isn't it great?" I said, excited that she had joined us.

She chuckled, but she was staring at me not at the castle.

"You better wash that off before it dries and hardens or you won't be able to move," she said. "An impressive castle, by the way. Need help?"

Just then, Dad walked out of the trees. He stopped when he saw Mum.

She opened her mouth but then snapped it shut. Whatever it was that had made her look bright and sunny drained off her face like the river water seeping into the muddy bank under my feet.

"Help us make a flag for the castle?" I said.

"Oh, no, I have dinner in the oven. Wouldn't want to burn it. I just came to check on you. I thought you were here alone."

She smiled at me like it was a secret code, only I didn't understand it. But she had lied, because as she turned to go back to the house, her swimsuit strap poked out from under her dress. I watched as she went up the path to where our house sat in the shade of the linden tree.

When I rushed in through the front door late that afternoon, Mum yelled through the open kitchen door, "Go clean yourself up before coming in here."

"Of course," I said although my foot was already in the kitchen doorway.

The tiles around me looked pink from the setting sun

as I showered. When I combed my hair, there was still some sand in it, but I couldn't be bothered to rinse it again. I messed it up a little so Mum wouldn't see how poorly I'd washed it.

I skipped down the stairs two steps at a time and ran straight into Dad, who was standing in the kitchen doorway.

"Slow down, Nina."

"Sorry, Dad."

He turned back to Mum. "So, I'll get the charcoal and the meat in the morning and then I can grill it out back. It'd be best if we ate inside because of the heat."

My mouth watered at the thought of grilled meat, reserved for special occasions.

"Sure," Mum said.

He turned to me. "And you two will make the cake. It better be good."

"The best," I said as I tied my apron.

Mum promised me ages ago I could help her make the cake for Grandpa's eightieth birthday. I had been looking forward to it so long, and now it was here at last. It was too hot during the day to bake. We waited until the sun went down so we could open the windows and doors to let the evening air into the house.

"You can beat the egg yolks and sugar," Mum said, and offered me the whisk.

The kitchen heated up as we whisked, mixed, melted butter, and sieved flour and baking powder.

"Do you know who taught me to bake cakes?" Mum asked after a while.

I shook my head.

"Grandpa."

"Really? I thought he only cooked pasta and polenta."

Mum laughed. "Really. Just before her tenth birthday, Marija fell ill. She spent two weeks in bed with a high fever. She threw up everything she ate. Grandpa thought it would cheer her up if we made a cake for her birthday. That was the first cake I remember anyone having for their birthday in the family."

"Did you manage to cheer her up?"

Mum poured the batter into the cake mould. She let me shake it to even it out, while she carried the empty bowl to the sink.

"I suppose. But as soon as she ate a piece of the cake, she threw up."

"That's a shame." All that baking for nothing.

"She did wake up feeling much better the next day, though," Mum said. She opened the oven for me to put the cake mould in. Carefully, I slid it onto the rack. I still had a mark on my arm from when I had burnt it on the oven door helping Mum make lasagne two months before.

"Sadly, it didn't last long."

"What didn't?"

She piled the dishes into the sink, and I pushed a stool to the worktop. She washed, and I rinsed. The clinking of pots and glasses was like a special tune that filled the kitchen every time Mum was in it.

"Marija's health. She fell ill again pretty soon after." Suddenly, Mum went silent.

I looked up to see Auntie Marija reflected in the glass of the darkened window above the sink.

"All finished?" Auntie Marija smiled when I turned to her.

"It just needs to bake. Then we'll make the filling," I said when Mum stayed silent.

"Chocolate?" Auntie Marija asked, staring at the large bar of dark chocolate on the worktop.

"And strawberries from the garden," I added.

"I can go pick them," she offered.

"It's all right, I'll do it," Mum said, not looking up from the dishes.

"Don't be silly, you're busy here. I may not be able to bake, but I can pick a few strawberries."

Auntie Marija took a bowl from the cupboard under the sink, forcing Mum to move to the side for a moment.

When she was out the door, Mum returned to washing, but her movements were sharp as if she was angry. I rinsed the last couple of glasses and one slipped from my fingers. The noise it made as it dropped into the sink rattled in my head.

Mum picked it up and inspected it. "It's whole. You were lucky. Or not."

"What?"

"If you break a glass, you'll have seven years of happiness," she explained.

Her words made so little sense I took a moment to think about it before I asked, "But wouldn't people break glasses on purpose if that were true?"

She stopped moving for a moment. "You can't force happiness."

I didn't know what to say to that, so I asked, "Why can't Auntie Marija bake?"

Mum wiped her hands and then handed the towel to me. Slowly, her face stretched into a smile. But then, as if trying to hide it, she shrugged. "She never learned."

I thought it strange that she sounded happy about it. But I was content that I was learning to bake and cook and that I could help Mum with more than just picking the strawberries in the garden.

By the time the filling was ready and the sponge cake sliced into two layers, sweat poured down my face. Bent low, Mum spread the filling evenly, adding the next layer on top and then finishing it off with the strawberry frosting. I looked on to learn everything I could.

Suddenly she stopped and stared at me.

"What?" I touched my cheek to check there wasn't any frosting. I had stolen some earlier but I thought I had covered my tracks well enough.

"You have sand in your hair, Nina."

"I have?"

She shook her head and went back to decorating the cake.

It was dark by the time Mum and I finished working. The kitchen was hot, but the breeze outside had cooled things down and fireflies flew about the garden. I was exhausted but excited that we would eat the cake the next day. I wondered if everyone would like it. But the most important thing was that I got to bake it with Mum. In the kitchen, she never frowned at me and scolded me.

Until I started school and I had to be part of school Shrovetide celebrations I had never put on a costume. I didn't understand why people enjoyed dressing in horrid getups. I didn't fear the masks people wore; it was more frightening that I couldn't see their real faces and tell who was behind the costumes.

On Shrove Saturday, I escaped to my room every time

a group of masks stopped at our house. I'd begged everyone not to open the doors and to pretend we weren't home.

"It brings bad luck to the house if you don't let the masks in," Grandpa said, as if it wasn't enough bad luck having odd people roam our home.

It had turned dark hours before and the wind blew outside. It was cold enough to freeze your ears and nose right off your head. Those celebrating Shrovetide would have their work cut out for them if they wanted to chase away winter.

Tired from worrying about it all day, I sat at the dinner table with Grandpa while Mum cleaned the worktops and put away the pots. Auntie Marija hadn't felt well and she stayed in her room. We were waiting for Dad to join us when the doorbell rang. I jumped up from my spot, knocking my plate so it slid across the table.

Grandpa laughed at me. "Where are you going?"

I dashed into the hallway, my heart hammering, but Dad was already at the front door. "Don't—" I started to say as panic shot through me.

Before I finished, the procession of masks burst through the door, crowding in on us in the small, dim hallway. There wasn't enough air for so many people in there.

Grandpa appeared in the kitchen doorway.

"Come on in." He gestured with his hand. "Through here."

It took forever for the group to trickle through the door into the kitchen. Mechanics with grease-stained hands, old hags with teeth painted rotten, furry creatures, and even a devil moved past me like a wave of ugliness and horror.

Just when I thought I was saved, Grandpa called, "Come on, Nina."

A few of the masks turned, staring at me. I was caught. I couldn't run now because I wasn't sure they wouldn't come after me and then I'd be alone in my room with no one to protect me from them. So I had to trust Dad's hand on my shoulder as he gently pushed me forwards. My feet itched with the need to flee. I wasn't sure how Dad managed to get me into the kitchen, but I knew he would be there if I needed him.

The room erupted with the sound of an accordion, washtub bass and washboard. Grandpa moved from one mask to the next, offering grappa. It was as though he'd been waiting the entire year for this moment.

I tried to make myself invisible, terrified that someone would notice me and come closer.

"What are you collecting?" Mum asked into the silence that followed the loud tune.

A tall man, dressed in a mechanic's costume and plastic face mask that covered even his hair, showed her the basket filled with doughnuts and eggs, a bottle, and a couple of salamis. Another man, dressed as an old, dreadful-looking woman—his big hands gave him away—jangled another, smaller basket covered with fabric with an opening in the centre. Coins tinkled inside and banknotes rustled. What would they do with the money—pay winter to go away?

The fridge door groaned as Mum took out a carton of eggs. She put them into the larger basket, standing as far away as she could. It seemed Grandpa was the only one enjoying this, so I couldn't understand why anyone else opened the door to let them in. In school, we were told it was superstitious to believe Shrovetide costumes brought good luck and warmer weather. If I knew that, how come my parents didn't?

"Another one?" Grandpa asked the man closest to him, lifting the grappa bottle, which was half empty by now. The man offered his glass and Grandpa filled it up, and then the next and the next.

The tune that followed was noisier than the previous one. The furry creature and someone wearing a gas mask started to twirl and sway. They stumbled and knocked into chairs. Several masks exploded in braying laughter and that made the whole thing even more horrible.

I shuddered and pressed my back to the wall and slipped behind Dad. Today it would have been a blessing to feel poorly like Auntie Marija and stay in my room.

My breath came a bit easier when people closest to the door turned to leave. They nodded their thanks and goodbyes, the words useless as the accordion was too loud to hear anything other than the out-of-tune sounds.

The Devil passed me on his way to the door and suddenly reached out and grabbed my arm. I screeched and jerked away but I could not escape. It was as if my terror excited them. Even the masks already out the door came back to watch as the Devil grabbed me and forced me to dance with him.

"Leave me alone," I tried to say calmly and with confidence, but it came out as a panicked cry.

The dark face high above me gave a laugh and it sounded hollow and ominous. I knew this was because his voice was trapped behind the wooden mask, yet my heart was about to burst out of my chest. He smelled of stale alcohol and ham.

My cheeks burned as I was dragged across the kitchen floor, stumbling and slumping.

I searched for someone to help me. Mum was in the hallway, holding the front door open. I could feel the chilly February air sneaking in, freezing my feet and making me more awkward.

Grandpa stood to the side, laughing and clapping to the rhythm as if this was the best fun he'd had in a long while. My last chance was Dad, but as I caught a glimpse of him when the Devil swung me around, he had an absent smile on his face.

By the time the Devil at last let me slip out of his grip, my hands were clammy and legs wobbly. I stumbled against the cupboards, grabbing the top for support.

The Devil's laugh sounded louder than the accordion as he walked out, glancing at me once more before he vanished into the dark nothing beyond the door. I didn't wait for the others to follow him.

"You shouldn't be so afraid of them," Dad said, his voice rising with the last words so I could hear him as I ran past.

Mum came up to my bedroom once the noise downstairs settled and the front door closed with a thud. "Stop being silly, Nina," she said.

I pressed my lips tighter together, hugging my teddy bear which was too threadbare to offer comfort.

"They're just costumes and masks," she tried again, her tone gentler.

"You don't understand anything." Angry and frustrated I was near tears, and that angered me more. I didn't need her to tell me it was just masks. I knew it was just masks and that was what I was afraid of.

"No, sometimes I don't. But I know this: there are things in life one must learn to put up with, Nina. You're nine, you're growing up. Fast. You'll need to toughen up."

Well, that was the stupidest thing to say. "What if I don't?"

Her forehead scrunched up. She sat on the edge of the bed, but she didn't try to reach out or hug me. I remembered how I had left for summer camp the year before. My classmates were laughing and talking in the car park behind the school. Parents walked around; some talked among themselves. When the time came to board buses, the entire car park hugged in one giant cuddle. I wondered how come my parents never hugged me like that.

Dad thought it important to emphasise again I was to obey the teachers and not cause trouble, while Mum stared across the car park, as if lost in thought. I caught the look of a girl from another class as she let go of her mum. She glanced at my parents and back at me. I was suddenly ashamed, of not being enough, of not being deserving of a hug. I threw myself at Mum with such force she swayed, only just catching her balance. I didn't wait for her to hug me back, too embarrassed and hurt. I picked up my bag and dragged it to the bus, forcing my way through the group of dads who'd helped the drivers load their children's luggage.

I hadn't looked back as I climbed onto the bus. I hadn't cried either. But Mum still thought I should toughen up. What if I didn't?

She sighed softly and said, "Then you'll be very miserable in life."

"Isn't there something happy to look forward to?" I couldn't understand why she was always so negative about everything.

"Sometimes the good things make you hurt the most."

"That's stupid," I shot back. "You're not making sense."

"Maybe, but it's the truth."

I stared at the window turned mirror against the dark outside. I wondered about the ugly masks wandering the streets at night. Who was behind them?

Mum's reflection in the glass caught my attention. Her profile was sharp but the colours were pale in the mirror image. She looked different, as if she was wearing a disguise, too. I felt her looking at me.

Moments later, she got up and left. She didn't wish me a good night and I was glad because if she didn't believe in good things, it would have been a lie. I could only hope she was wrong.

FOUR

On a warm autumn day when the sun through the window lit up the kitchen, Auntie Marija again didn't join us for lunch. I offered to take her plate up to her room, but Mum took it herself. It was a while before she returned. Her face was drawn and even her hair was messier than before.

She piled the dirty dishes from lunch into the sink and then took half of them out again because it was too full.

"Get out of the way, Nina," she muttered when she bumped into me as I carried the bread basket to the worktop.

I walked backwards towards the door, ready to flee. It wasn't fair she complained when I was trying to help.

A plate slipped from her hands and crashed to the floor, creating a jumble of shards. It was almost like the mosaic we had made in the playground the month before.

I didn't understand a thing any more. Mum had never been a cheerful, smiling person, but she was becoming even more nervous and exhausted. She was easily distracted, leaving her chores half done, and even complained about Grandpa being messy and forgetful, which she had never done before. If only someone else were here now in case Mum lost her temper so I wouldn't be the obvious target, but lately, everyone scattered as soon as we finished eating. I used to like how our kitchen was the most crowded place in the house, but Dad rarely came in these days except for mealtimes, and Auntie Marija and Grandpa stayed in their rooms in the attic.

I'd hide in my bedroom, too, but the quietness made my thoughts too loud. It was difficult to choose between that and the uneasy feel of the kitchen as Mum's changes of mood seemed to be getting more frequent.

Mum waved me over then. "Come with me."

"Where are we going?"

She didn't answer me but when she smiled, I followed her. She stepped out of the house and kept walking towards the river. I wanted to ask if I needed to put on my shoes, but she didn't wait long enough.

My breathing was fast because of our quick pace and the dampness that made the air heavy and syrupy. Long, late-afternoon shadows crept along the valley and the rushing of the river was louder with each step.

The swimming season was over, but that didn't stop Mum kicking off her shoes and wading into the chilly water.

"Mum?" I said.

She looked at me as if she'd only just noticed I had followed her. Her smile looked a little sad. "It's all right. It's not that cold," she said in a comforting tone. She waded along the shore.

On the bank, I wrapped my arms around myself. The coldness of the stones chilled my feet through the thin soles of my slippers. I wondered how she wasn't freezing.

Mum's back looked strangely broken when she bent, dipping her fingers into the river. I yelped at how cold the droplets were when she splashed me. I laughed, surprised.

I hadn't seen her so carefree in a long time. At least since that last time she had allowed me to help cook pasta with ragout a few weeks before.

We sat side by side on the bank. Mum gathered the wet hem of her apron in her hands to wring out the water.

My eyes were glued to the blue veins on Mum's legs, her see-through skin, so different to my smooth complexion. How old was she? Ancient. Older than most mums who came to school assemblies. I had never thought about her age before, but worrying about Auntie Marija made Mum seem older. She became quieter, and sometimes she would just stare into space. It scared me because it was like she could see things I couldn't. She would gaze out of the kitchen window and when she heard me coming, she pretended she was wiping the glass or fixing the curtains but she only made the glass dirtier.

I lay back on the grassy bank and stared at the leaves of a tree and the sky above. The clouds moved, giving the impression the sky was passing by, going on to other places while everything here stayed the same. The valley was so narrow it appeared to trap us. I wondered if this small, limited space made Mum feel safe because it was familiar. I felt as if the air was being squeezed out of me by the tall mountains, the overgrown forest on the slopes. I envied the river its freedom to leave this place. I wanted to follow it and see where it took me.

The furthest I had been was the few kilometres across the border to Italy. We mostly shopped for jeans and coffee, always making sure we didn't buy too much because the customs officers marked every purchase in our border passes. I missed going to the fair, but Mum and Dad no longer offered to take me. It had been ages since

I last went with them to Italy. Was it in May? Certainly long before the summer holidays. In June they went again, but that time, they left me with Grandpa and Auntie Marija.

The day before their trip, I'd overheard Mum talking to Dad in the hallway. "She can stay home," she had said. "We'll just buy some coffee and chocolate. We don't need her border pass this time."

When they left the next day, I asked Grandpa what Mum had meant, and he explained that once we had used up the allotted amount of imported goods, we wouldn't be able to bring anything for several months. "You need more border passes for bigger purchases," he'd said.

So even my border pass couldn't get me out of this valley any more. Everything conspired against me: my parents, border control, even the landscape. But the greater the obstacles, the more I wanted to know what was beyond those tall mountains.

Every afternoon when I returned from school, Auntie Marija used to prepare me a snack before my parents finished work and then we would have dinner. But for weeks, it was Grandpa who welcomed me home. It wasn't that I didn't love him just as much as Auntie Marija, but he never gave me chocolate and he put very little jam on my bread. Whenever I asked where Auntie Marija was, he mumbled and nodded in the general direction of her attic room. No one told me anything and I wasn't supposed to disturb her so I imagined she was still unwell.

When I came home from school the last day before the holidays started in November, our house felt different. It had always been a quiet house but that day the silence was heavier. Before I could find out what was going on, Mum stopped me in the downstairs hallway and led me up to my bedroom.

"Sit," she said.

I obeyed because there was something in Mum's eyes, as if she was begging me not to cause trouble. Had I done something wrong at school? I couldn't remember any offence that could make her look so serious. I had forgotten to do my homework two weeks before, but she'd have heard about it long before now.

"There's something I need to tell you." Her expression frightened me.

The sounds of something heavy being moved downstairs distracted me as I tried to focus on Mum's words. I stared at her grim face and thought of Mum and Dad's behaviour in the past few months. Of how they had avoided each other, not speaking for days, Mum sending me with messages for Dad and him doing the same.

Would she tell me they were splitting up? I hadn't known parents could do that, until last year when Martin's parents had divorced, and it took the entire class a month to understand what that meant. But Martin was okay. So I supposed I would be, too. When I had asked him, he said his mum and dad barely spoke to each other. It sounded familiar. I had thought my parents' never-ending silences were because Auntie Marija was ill, so Mum had more work to do and was tired and grumpy because of it. But perhaps it had nothing to do with Auntie Marija; perhaps it was all down to Mum and Dad.

"Nina, Auntie Marija is gone."

"Where did she go?"

Mum grimaced. Her hands were clasped, her fingers

turning white. Something didn't add up. "Did she get worse?" I asked. "Was she taken to hospital?" The possibility of having no one to play with during the holidays made me sad.

There were red patches on Mum's cheeks and there was something frightening in the way she was standing. She looked just like Grandpa when he struggled to stand straight and tall as old age pulled him towards the ground.

"She's gone, Nina. She died," Mum said, and I almost didn't hear her because she whispered the words.

I stared at her. Mum was trembling. All the words in my mind scattered and I remained silent.

She cleared her throat and her voice was almost back to normal when she said, "Will you be all right on your own for an hour?"

There were so many things that baffled me I couldn't answer straight away. All right? On my own? Even time confused me. Had it been five minutes or five hours since I got home?

I would turn ten in January. I was almost grown up and I should know these things, so I did what grown-ups did.

"Yes," I lied.

Later that afternoon, Grandpa stopped all the clocks in the house. I asked him why, and he blinked his watery eyes and said, "Time has stopped for your aunt." Then he wiped his mouth with his handkerchief as if too embarrassed to wipe his eyes. He hadn't shaved and the deep valleys in his cheeks were speckled with grey stubble. He looked confused when he closed the glass door of the grandfather clock as if he didn't know where to go or what to do next. At last, he walked out the front door in his slippers and shirtsleeves.

I had no idea where everyone else was as I sat at the kitchen table. I suspected Mum was in the living room because I heard movement and smelled candles burning. Was Auntie Marija in there, too? Mum had said there would be a wake. I had asked what a wake was and she said people would come to say goodbye to Auntie Marija. What was the point when she couldn't hear them any longer? Would I have to say goodbye too? I'd never seen a dead person. I had seen dead fish Dad sometimes brought from the market. I could never bring myself to look at their sightless little eyes. He'd told me fishermen whacked them on the head to spare them the suffering once they removed them from the water. My stomach churned at the memory and my thumb hurt as I bit my nail to the quick.

The front door opened and closed, and the next second, Mrs Vidic came into the kitchen. Against the black skirt and jacket and a grey-black silk shawl her skin was sallow, but her movements were quick as if she were younger than when I had last seen her.

"Poor little Nina."

I flinched when she reached me in three long strides. Her bony fingers squeezed my shoulder, and I sank deeper in the chair, my face barely above the table now.

"Where's your mother?" she asked, her eyes glancing around the room as if she suspected Mum was hiding in a cupboard.

"I—" I cleared my throat when the words stuck. "I think she's in the living room," I whispered.

More people arrived soon after. Mrs Vidic let them in and showed them into the living room.

I was both grateful no one came to talk to me and

terrified because I was left alone in the kitchen. Every time a door opened or closed I jumped on the uncomfortable chair. Would I have to join them in the living room? How did you say goodbye to a dead person? Did you talk to them? But the grown-ups would laugh at that, surely?

"You're still here?" Mrs Vidic asked when she returned after some time. She started opening the cupboards. From a bottom cupboard, she heaved up the largest pot she could find and filled it with water. Her next search produced a box of herbal teas Mum gathered and dried every summer for use during winter.

"Go get dressed," she said, without looking at me.

"Dressed?" I stammered.

"Your Sunday clothes, dear. Your trousers are torn at the knee. You can't wear that when people come."

Did that mean more people would come? The horrible feeling in my stomach got stronger. I didn't know what to make of all the feelings in me and I didn't know how to deal with strangers coming to our house. I wanted to be left alone.

I went upstairs in a daze. What did Mrs Vidic have in mind when she said Sunday clothes? My favourite was a blue and red dress with a beautiful, flowing skirt, which I'd only worn once. I thought of Mrs Vidic's all-black clothing. She probably hadn't meant for me to wear a pretty dress. After staring into the wardrobe so long Mrs Vidic called my name from the stairs in a forced whisper, I hurriedly pulled on the grey trousers and a thin polo neck I wore to school.

Mrs Vidic grasped my hand in hers, her other hand occupied with a tray of teacups, and led me into the living room.

The room was dim, with the curtains closed and the lights off, but the candles were brilliant. The air smelled of incense and strange people's perfumes. After just a few moments it suffocated me.

Dad and Grandpa weren't in the living room. I felt more alone than in the kitchen earlier. Mrs Vidic pushed me onto the bench next to my mother and then she sat on my other side. Her bony elbow poked into my ribs. Four people sat on chairs facing the bench. I recognised their faces but I couldn't remember all their names. All four of them turned to stare at me, smiling sadly. Their attention made me feel so weird I nearly bolted.

The old sewing machine from the corner was gone, and only a dark line from where the wooden top rubbed against the wall remained. The fabric hanging over the small mirror by the door was about to slip off. My fingers itched to fix it, even though I didn't know why the mirror had been covered in the first place.

My eyes kept going to the coffin, pushed up against the far wall. I worried that Auntie Marija was uncomfortable because the coffin was made of wood. But the lid was open and white fabric flowed over the sides, so I guessed she at least had a pillow in there. Standing on a sort of table, it was so high I could only just see a lock of hair on her forehead. The two candles at the lower end flickered, the hissing carrying in the silent room. A framed photograph of Auntie Marija sat on a low table next to the coffin. I'd never seen it before. Even in the dim light, the face on it looked nothing like the quiet aunt I had known. Her eyes sparkled. Maybe it was just the candlelight that did that. Her eyes would never open again. How was that possible? She would never again read me *The Princess and the Pea* and then giggle as we imagined what it would be like to be a princess. I wouldn't be able to go to her room to play with the straw doll she'd given me. Her seat at the kitchen table would be left empty.

I wiped at the wetness on my hand, surprised by the tears. As more people walked in, I couldn't face them. I didn't want them to see my tear-stained cheeks. None of the grown-ups cried.

Auntie Marija had been feeling poorly for a while. I'd asked Mum what it was that she had died of, and all she said was, "She was unwell."

Well, of course she was, but Grandpa constantly complained about feeling poorly, too, and he was still alive. People didn't die of feeling unwell. She probably had some horrible disease. Perhaps it was contagious and that was why she had stayed in her room and why no one wanted to talk about it. But someone else might have caught it, too. Maybe even me. I held my breath at the thought of what would happen to me if I had. My stomach churned and I felt light-headed.

Despite all the people in it, the room was cold. It was slowly getting louder and I even heard laughter from time to time. Mum shook hands and kissed cheeks and nodded at the words people whispered to her, but she looked distant and strangely confused, her eyes moving around the room.

Perhaps she, too, wished she could be somewhere else.

Mrs Vidic took hold of my hand and pulled me up from my seat. Mum's hand grabbed my other arm to stop me. "I want her to stay."

"I thought perhaps some tea would do her good," Mrs Vidic said, gesturing to my shivering. I hugged myself for emphasis.

"Bring more in," Mum said, handing Mrs Vidic the empty tray.

Mrs Vidic stared at Mum. Hesitating, she then said, "Nelida, it's all over now."

But Mum just glared at her and then glanced at me for a moment.

I couldn't believe Mum wouldn't let me leave the room, even if just for a little while. I felt ill from the sweet smells of perfumes, flowers, and the candles. The room was thick with it and I needed fresh air. Besides, Dad and Grandpa weren't there. How come they were allowed to avoid it all while I had to put up with strange eyes watching me and people I didn't know patting my head, telling me it would be all right? What did they know?

Mrs Vidic muttered but didn't argue. I took that as a sign I would be wise not to insist either, so I sat back down as Mrs Vidic escaped out the door. The wait for the tea went on forever, and when I couldn't sit still any more, I whispered to Mum, "Bathroom." Let her try to stop me.

Once I closed the bathroom door behind me, the silence and absence of people was so sudden I almost missed the sounds. I couldn't believe there was a spot in the house as quiet as this. I breathed in and closed my eyes when tears threatened again. I felt all wonky. I didn't understand what the purpose of all this was. Auntie Marija couldn't know whether we said goodbye, anyhow. She was dead.

I washed my face. Instead of calming me, it just made me shiver more.

On a peg on the door, Auntie Marija's cardigan, which she'd worn so often I wondered if she perhaps missed it even now, still swang back and forth from when I had closed the door. I put it on over my polo neck and immediately felt warmer.

In the kitchen, I found Mrs Vidic pouring tea into cups.

"Your mum's really upset. You shouldn't resent her," she said without looking up.

I dropped into a chair by the range. "It's so strange. People are talking in there as if nothing has happened, and Auntie Marija is lying right next to them." I didn't know how I had imagined saying goodbye to someone when they died, but it wasn't like this. I hadn't expected strangers to show up. I had thought it would be just us. I didn't even want Mrs Vidic to be there. I remembered how she once said that Auntie Marija had been a nuisance for my parents because they had to support her. I didn't think someone who said things like that really cared about people.

She looked shocked when she turned to me and saw the cardigan. "Nina! Take that off. And you shouldn't talk like that, it's not proper."

"I'm cold, and I'll talk any way I like." I was so miserable the words just sprang out of me. How was I doing anything wrong when there were people chatting and laughing next to a dead body? This seemed all so wrong. Auntie Marija dying, Mum being even more bad-tempered than usual, Mrs Vidic taking over the house. And Dad wasn't even there to set things right, to do something. I wanted things to go back to normal but I didn't even know what that was.

Mrs Vidic pressed her lips, but she didn't look angry. I wondered if she would send me to my room to calm down or force me to go back into the crowded room across the hall. The low buzz of voices from the living room reached the kitchen. My skin crawled and my entire being vibrated with the monotonous sound.

"It will be all right," she said.

I bit back the "No, it won't" because I didn't know if she was right or not.

I reached for a cup of tea, but her hand stopped me. Her cheeky smile when she picked up a bottle from the table, uncapped it, and poured a few drops of the liquid into the tea surprised me so much my mouth fell open.

"This'll warm you up," she whispered.

I hated the pong of grappa, but mixed with the smell of the anise tea, it wasn't so bad. I drank the tea in one gulp, and it warmed me up.

I didn't like feeling grateful to Mrs Vidic, who I'd disliked as long as I could remember, so I escaped from the kitchen and ran straight into Grandpa and Dad in the hallway.

I didn't dare speak; I was terrified they would smell the alcohol on my breath. Grandpa stared at me but he had a faraway look. His face was like the slabs of stone under our feet: grey, hard, and old. Without a word, he turned and walked out the front door.

Dad blinked his red-rimmed eyes and said, "Mum needs you now." Before I could answer, he left through the back door.

When Mum saw me, the words stumbled on her lips and her eyes turned cold as they looked up and down my body, seeing my borrowed cardigan.

I sat in my spot, ignoring the warning in her eyes, as I pulled the cardigan tighter around me. I was so furious with her, with everyone, and I didn't even know why.

In between welcoming visitors, she managed to hiss, "For Christ's sake, what are you wearing?"

Her irritation gave me satisfaction. "It's cold in here, and if you're making me stay…"

She bit her lip. Scolding me in front of everyone would be bad manners. But her hand grabbed my arm, and I regretted being so difficult. If this was hard for me, it was probably harder for Mum.

It was past ten at night by the time Mrs Vidic realised I should have been in bed already. I was glad to go upstairs, but I couldn't sleep. People kept coming and going through the night. Every time I was almost asleep the front door woke me when it closed with a bang. I guessed that was why it was called a wake.

My eyes burned with tiredness the next morning. I ate my breakfast in the corner by the range as the kitchen was now full of people, too. I swallowed the hard lumps of bread, staring into my cocoa to avoid their eyes. Someone cried and snivelled. Mrs Vidic walked past me and asked, "Are you all right?"

I nodded but I felt awful. I hadn't seen Mum or Dad since the day before. Grandpa came into the kitchen, dressed in a dark suit I had never seen before. He poured himself grappa and walked back out. He didn't speak to anyone.

Dad appeared in the doorway. "We're ready," he said.

People rose from their chairs.

I wasn't ready. I needed more time. To do what, I didn't know.

Mrs Vidic took hold of my arm and pulled me after her. Outside, she pushed me through the people to the front. Mum stood next to the coffin, which was on a trolley. Her eyes were red, her cheeks blotchy. My eyes stung and I tried hard not to cry.

"You'll walk with your mum and dad," Mrs Vidic said, and pushed me towards Mum. I didn't know how I had thought we would get to the cemetery, but I hadn't thought we would go on foot.

The walk went on forever. The patent leather of my shoes chafed my heels. My hand went numb from Mum's tight hold on it.

Everything was said and done quietly, until we reached the cemetery and the gate creaked. Six men lifted the coffin off the trolley. It leaned sideways, and I gasped, terrified it would fall. It was only when we stood by the newly dug grave that I let my breath out. A choir sang as people moved in closer. A man walked up to the grave afterwards. I didn't know him and I didn't listen to what he was saying.

When the funeral was over, Mum and Dad, Grandpa, and Mrs Vidic and I walked back home. The house felt empty after two days of so many people being there. The silence made the house seem bigger somehow. I'd lived in it my whole life but now it seemed strange.

It went on like that for a week, silent and odd, until I couldn't stand it and I went and knocked on Grandpa's door.

"Tell me a story, Grandpa," I asked, but he didn't move from the window or give any sign he'd heard me.

"From when you were little. Please, Grandpa." Having to beg him was like being punished for something I hadn't done. I had never had to beg him before for stories. I didn't even ask him to tell me a story about Auntie Marija; any story would do. As long as someone talked to me.

"I've seen too much of the world to like it any more," he said. "Stories are lies. That's what they are. Rotten lies."

Grandpa had always been kind to me. He'd only ever hurt me once. I was four, and I was doodling on the kitchen table with my colouring pens. Grandpa slapped my hand when I wouldn't stop even after he'd told me to. I still remembered the stinging pain on my skin. I felt it now too, only it stung in my chest, just under my collarbone.

The quiet went on for weeks. My parents and Grandpa behaved so differently to before. Whenever I mentioned Auntie Marija, they stared into space and looked unhappy. I missed her; I wanted to talk about her. Mum left the kitchen once, wiping her eyes with a hankie, after I'd asked if Auntie Marija could see us still. I stopped mentioning her after that even though I felt there was a hole in my heart where she used to be.

I was afraid that if I disturbed Mum's silence, something in her would crack, break beyond repair. But I couldn't talk to Dad because I didn't see him for days, and when he did appear, it felt as though he left as soon as he saw me. I started looking forward to school days to get out of the house and speak to people who didn't know sadness.

A month after the funeral, Mum returned to work even though she seemed ill and tired. Grandpa looked as if he'd aged a dozen years and he acted as if I no longer existed. I felt lost even where I should've been most comfortable and at home. Mum started cleaning out

Auntie Marija's room. I wished I'd taken the straw doll before Mum threw everything away.

As a little girl, I used to fall asleep with a baby blanket Auntie Marija had made for me, but now I cried a little every night when I held it against my cheek. Maybe Mum felt the same way about Auntie Marija's things, which was why she got rid of them. But I still thought it wrong that everything to do with Auntie Marija disappeared from the house. Wouldn't that make us forget her and shouldn't we fight against it?

Auntie Marija had been so quiet and invisible that even her absence was more starkly noticed than she had ever been. As though she was more present by not being present.

FIVE

The strip blind in Mrs Vidic's open door dances in the lazy breeze as if trying to seduce flies, not drive them away. A clanging comes from somewhere deep in the house.

"Mrs Vidic?" I call into the dimness.

The woman was half deaf decades ago, so the absence of a reply is no surprise.

I call out again as I take tentative steps down the dark hallway. I don't want to barge in. Then I realise Mrs Vidic would never think of it that way. She would expect visitors to just come in. That's how things are done here, different from Paris or Melbourne where I make sure I lock my door whenever I'm inside my apartment.

It isn't the first time that it strikes me how much more normal and practical my parents' generation was—still is. But it's in my nature to complicate things. Where has that come from? I haven't inherited the trait from my parents, who considered earth, sand, and a water hose to be the most entertaining and educational toys for me when I was little.

"Here you are, then," a voice sounds from the darkness.

I squint at the stooped figure in the doorway to my right.

"You scared me," I say, exhaling.

"I heard you'd come back." Her voice vibrates with

scorn.

"From whom?" I ask.

The old woman looks at me sideways and crosses the hallway. I needn't have asked. Everyone knows everyone here. By now, the whole village probably knows my bathroom sink clogged up this morning. Welcome home.

"I came for my father," I say when the silence drags on.

"Took you long enough."

I won't make excuses. "I thought I'd stop by and see how you're doing, Mrs Vidic."

"Eh, can't you see? My bones are dead tired. The smell of soil is clinging to me already. I don't know what's taking so long. It's time."

She has lived alone for as long as I can remember. I have no clue how old she is. My mother told me she had once had a son. I pieced together the rest from gossip. There was a grandchild. Mrs Vidic was convinced his parents weren't taking good enough care of him. She reported them to social services. In doing so, she didn't just lose her son but her grandchild, too. I never heard what happened to her husband.

Mrs Vidic babysat me on a few occasions and I don't remember those times with joy. It wasn't above her to slap me if she thought I merited it. I got a few bruises from the encounters with the stubborn, angry woman, but it wasn't as though I could complain to my parents.

The old woman standing in front of me now, shrivelled and shrunken in on herself, as much emotionally as physically, is a scarred soul. For decades, she has cohabited with her resentment in a house too small for both of them.

"You'll be here for many more years. You don't smell of

soil, you smell of lemon." I try to sound encouraging.

"That's from the cleaning products I was using. I just washed my chamber pot." She plods through into the kitchen, and I follow.

The sun filters through the vine trellis outside the kitchen window, bathing the room in a greenish light. Even the heavy table and the two scuffed chairs were painted green once upon a time. The glass panes of the beige cupboard are covered with cracked brown newspaper. I examine the articles. They sound alien, with the old, formal language which lacks the sensationalism of today's media. In this kitchen, the language belongs.

There isn't a single family photograph anywhere. I finger the phone in my pocket, feeling weak and self-indulgent for holding on to the two snapshots I have of Yves. I captured him once as he cooked in my kitchen in Paris. The other was of him standing on my balcony in Melbourne, drinking strong black coffee mere hours before we ended our relationship for the second time. The expression on his face, which I thought looked calm and poised, appears sad in retrospect. Maybe he had sensed what was coming and it upset him more than I had thought.

"Tea or grappa?" Mrs Vidic asks.

"Just some tea, thanks," I say, because it's rude to decline. But I can't imagine drinking anything right now. Vomiting all over her floor might be even ruder.

I thought she would make a fresh pot. Instead, she pours a pale liquid from a pot on the wood-burning stove. I peer into the cup. Leafy bits float in the lukewarm drink. An unappetising film forms on the surface almost immediately.

My mouth fills with saliva and I have trouble swallowing. The room acquires an overwhelming smell of decay. I bite the inside of my cheeks to stop me salivating. I down the tea in one gulp.

"You seem thirsty. Would you care for some more?"

The tea tasted of mouldy hay. I shake my head, teeth clamped, just in case.

Mrs Vidic gestures to my hair as I push it behind my ear. "You don't look like you any more. You're the same as everyone else."

"I beg your pardon?"

"Your hair. You used to wear it short, like a boy. You never combed it. You had a fit once when I tried to neaten it. You've changed," she reproaches me.

"I grew up, Mrs Vidic," I say. "We all change."

"Not always for the better. And call me Silva, please."

"True," I say, if only to appease her.

In the sunlit kitchen, the purple bags underneath Silva's eyes are accentuated. The exhaustion and old age they suggest is in stark contrast to the glint in her eyes. Silva has always given the impression she knows about everything going on in the village, including in our house. That's why I've come to see her although I don't even know what to ask her or what I expect to find out.

"I've been to see my father in hospital," I say. "He's changed, too."

"Well, what do you expect with a disease like that?" Silva interrupts.

"He hasn't told me." My defensiveness screams guilt because I haven't bothered to ask him either. "Anyway, I just wanted to know how long he's been like this, I suppose. Has he told you about the cancer? Because he never mentioned…" My voice breaks and I don't know what to say anyhow. Too late, I wish I had been more involved in his life, but I have no idea what his last weeks and months at home have been like. It was a terrible idea to come to Silva to ask her about it. It just makes me look like an awful daughter and even more pathetic than I feel.

"He hasn't," she says, "but I've noticed the changes. Small ones, at first, but recently he started forgetting my name and other things, or he would talk about past events as though they happened yesterday. It's no surprise, though, that he hasn't told you."

I look up.

"He said you were some grand chef like the ones you see on the telly. He was proud of you. Said that was Nelida's doing because you certainly didn't inherit it. I suppose he didn't want to disrupt your career." Silva drops her gaze to the cup in her lap.

"Did he say that?"

Silva doesn't answer. The wrinkled skin of her face folds like shutters over her expression. She doesn't look old when she abruptly stands and steps towards me, her arms wide as if trying to shoo me out. She stops short of making the shooing sound, but the gestures are all there. The unexpected change surprises me and before I can think of anything to say, I find myself at the door.

I cross the road in shock over her sudden brusqueness. She has always been anything but polite, but the abrupt switch from telling me that my father was proud of me to sending me away is unusual even for her.

I set about cooking dinner, but I'm too distracted. The eggs burn. I think of our small, isolated family with no living relatives I know of. Just the thought of having to go to Silva to talk about my father makes me sad. I never knew my father's parents; both died before I was born. So, besides Marija, I only knew Grandpa, who died almost fifteen years ago. God, I can't believe it's been that long.

I throw the charred eggs in the bin and change my plans. Remembering Grandpa, I decide to make *paštašuta*, as he called the dish. The name was wrongly used because it derived from *pasta asciutta*, dried pasta. How Grandpa came to associate it with this dish, I don't know.

When I was little, Grandpa would tell me stories every chance he got; they were mostly war stories. But he shared his history with me, unlike my parents, and so he made me feel wanted and accepted.

He would peel the potatoes, trying to keep the peel in one long strip. He and his older brothers used to compete to see who would end up with the longest single piece, he told me. He won every time. It was all about patience and precision. "Remember that," he said. "Both are important if you want to succeed." His gaze would cloud over and the peel would break with the moment of inattention. "Of course, I never made much of myself. Didn't get the chance, with the war and all. We didn't starve, though, the girls and me. We didn't starve."

They hadn't had pasta back when my mother and Marija were young. He cooked it years later, when the girls were in school and their mother had already died of pneumonia. Marija loved it, but Nelida thought it was too simple, he said.

Listening to him talking about my mother and aunt as girls, it was as if he were talking about strangers. I couldn't imagine my mother as a girl my age because she was nothing like me.

Chuckling, Grandpa assured me that, indeed, my mother was once but a girl.

He would cook the diced potatoes and pasta in separate pots and simmer tiny pieces of bacon and then add shop-bought tomato sauce from a tube. Half a spoon of the concentrate and the entire dish would taste of tomatoes. Magic back then, cheap, poor-quality stuff I wouldn't want to use in my kitchen today.

I strain the potatoes and pasta. On top, I pour some of the leftover sauce I made from fresh tomatoes the day before. The smell reminds me of childhood.

I always suspected Grandpa was particularly protective of my aunt, although he loved both his girls. My mother could take better care of herself. The flighty, dreamy Marija floated through life without a course or an anchor. Sometimes I resembled her in that respect, especially after every failed relationship when I felt as though I wasn't good enough.

It's a frightening thought that she was only thirty-seven when she died, barely eight years older than I am now. How could a life end so early? How could a life be left so unfulfilled?

I remember the black birds dipping their shadows onto the churchyard as they headed towards the snow-capped Alps on the day we buried her. They came to take Auntie Marija's soul with them, I thought, for safekeeping.

I was baffled by the whispers and talk behind moist handkerchiefs. My mother was swallowed up in commiserating glances and assurances that she couldn't have changed anything.

"These things happen."

"There's nothing you could've done."

"So sad, so young. It's an illness."

Even Grandpa once said, tapping his finger to his sunken temple, "She's not right in the head. Poor child." His eyes would turn even more watery than usual when he spoke like that.

I can't remember what I thought it was that Marija died of. I probably imagined a type of flu attacking her brain until it dissolved into snot. It wasn't anything specific; it certainly wasn't any one person telling me the truth. In my family, discovering things has always meant putting together a patchwork of conversations and eavesdropped bits, guesses and gut feelings. But by the time I reached my teens and fought my own battle with depression, I began to understand Aunt Marija had committed suicide. Depression was her disease.

It still shocks me how no one even thought of helping her. People would say depression was an illness, but no one really looked at it that way. They saw it as a shameful secret no one gave its proper name, but they couldn't make it go away by calling it something else.

Sitting on the hard, dry soil of the garden, I stare at the dark summer sky. The windows of the house gleam with the reflection of the stars and the silver sickle of the moon. The darkness is loud with creatures that have awoken after the heat of the day. The night-time smells of lavender, rosemary, lemon balm, and basil seem more pungent, but somehow melancholy.

I sometimes slept under the stars as a child, in the tent my father had pitched. My mother protested that lying outside at night wasn't good for my health. After my parents went to bed, I slipped out of the tent and made my bed next to the rosemary bush.

Tonight is the night St Lawrence sheds his starry tears. "Make a wish, make a wish," my aunt would say, excited when I caught a falling star. Every time, I made a wish, but nothing came true. Then I learned in Geography it was just rocks glowing when they hit the Earth's atmosphere. Still, I made a wish when I saw one, always hopeful this time it would be different. But the stars remained rocks even though my wishes were more and more desperate.

A spark flames now and slips through the sky like a droplet down the curve of a wine glass. No wish comes to me. Even if it had, I'd rather wish it upon a stream than a rock. Streams are alive and go places. Rocks are just inert burdens.

I think about the burdens Marija carried. How desperate she must have been if she saw no way out. I wonder if she had many sleepless nights, memories and worries keeping her awake like they're keeping me awake now.

I remember playing cards with her once and I complained about having to go to bed when I wasn't at all tired. I must have been around seven or eight and I had to get up early for school.

"Oh, child, if I could sleep, I'd go to bed with you," Auntie Marija said in her soft voice.

"Why can't you sleep?"

"Whenever I'm awake in someone else's dreams, I can't sleep," she said.

"Really?" It sounded magical to my gullible ears. I wondered who was dreaming about my aunt and keeping her awake.

"Mmm. Whenever you can't sleep, Nina, love, just know you're awake in my dreams."

I smiled when she pinched my chin.

In whose dreams am I awake at one in the morning on a warm summer night? I think of Yves, of the many nights we kept each other awake. Remembering the first time I met him at cookery school, it seems impossible we ended up in a relationship at all. He was so arrogant and insolent I considered dropping out. So many times during that first year, I wanted to scream in his face from frustration. But he got under my skin and I miss even his worst habits now.

I had started cooking after my mother died, but I never dreamed I'd become a chef. Cooking was something my mother and I shared, one of the rare things. I wasn't sure why I had returned to cooking after years of avoiding it since leaving home, but it all began when I returned home for my mother's funeral.

Ståle and I had been on our way home from a holiday when my father called to tell me my mother was ill. In Frankfurt, I rushed to change my plane tickets. I boarded a plane home alone, afraid of what I would find. The taxi from the airport to my parents' village cost me a fortune but I was in a hurry. I couldn't believe I was still too late. I saw it on my father's face when he opened the door. His eyes were bloodshot and his trembling lip when he tried to greet me made me feel awful.

We stood there facing each other as though we weren't sure who the other person was. We hadn't seen each other for five years. At last, he said, "Your mother…" His voice broke, and I could no longer look at his face. I reached for my suitcase, and he moved out of my way so I could enter.

The acrid smell hit me first. "Is something burning?"

When he rushed into the kitchen, I dropped the suitcase and followed him. The familiarity of the room shocked and disorientated me. I'd spent the flight home imagining the worst outcome of my mother's illness, but none of those dark thoughts were as sorrowful and real as the sight in front of me. Dirty dishes were piled in the sink, the cupboard fronts were dusty, and the worktop was strewn with crumbs, spilled milk, and grease—all proof my mother was no longer able to take care of her beloved kitchen. Although we hadn't parted on the best of terms, something in me crumbled when I saw this sign of her decline. The last vestiges of a dream of a home had vanished.

As sharp as this feeling of grief was, it was not the most pressing matter. On the kitchen table, covered with a blanket, my father's suit was spread out with the iron sitting on top. Dark, thick smoke was rising from the fabric. By the time I reached him, my father had already removed the iron and was patting the charred fabric with his bare hand. I wet the closest dish towel and handed it to him. Instead of placing it flat onto the fabric, he made a mess by rubbing the smoking patch until the damaged fabric gave way and tore.

"*Jebemti*," he swore, his face like thunder. "It's my only suit."

I stared at the sad remnants of the jacket. The damage was insignificant considering what he would need the suit for. "Where is Mum? I should go see her." My voice sounded alien.

My father's eyes drifted past me through the open

kitchen door and across the hall.

The living room, too, was dusty, a spiderweb spread in the corner by the door. No one had bothered to cover the mirror this time. A white lace-trimmed cloth covered the bier; the coffin lay open upon it.

Dread made my feet heavy and my heart fluttered in my chest. I'd grieved before but always with a childlike innocence. I neared the coffin and saw my mother's waxy face, her forever closed eyes, the hair styled in a way she had never worn it in life, and this time my grief wasn't as pure. It was tangled up with guilt and remorse and questions. Had I caused this by abandoning them? Should I have swallowed my own pain and stayed for their sake?

Instead of praying, I stood there, swaying slightly, going through these questions as though they were beads on a rosary. I couldn't say goodbye with so much unanswered. I could barely look at her even though she couldn't see the remorse on my face. My hand shook as I reached to touch her but I couldn't. I smoothed out the sleeve of her dress instead and then snatched my hand back.

I turned to see my father in the doorway. I hoped he hadn't witnessed that.

"She was peaceful at the end," he whispered, his eyes on my mother.

I wasn't sure I wanted to know this, to hear of her last moments, of the life they'd lived without me. "That's a relief," I said, because it was expected of me.

I spent the next hour trying to patch the tear in the side of my father's dark grey jacket. He inspected my work, his face falling when he saw what an awful job I had done. He sighed and said, "I wore it at our wedding. And when your grandpa died, and Marija. And now…"

He blew his nose in a crumpled handkerchief. He seemed poorly and shorter than I remembered him. Thin and grey. No one would notice the mended jacket when he looked such a mess.

People started pouring into our house, and I felt just as intruded on as when my aunt and Grandpa had died. My suitcase waited in the kitchen corner to be unpacked while I made tea and served it with stale biscuits. When those ran out, I threw together ingredients for my mother's favourite coffee cake. The routine of baking came to me shockingly easy and it kept my mind off the gathering mourners and my dead mother. I told myself this was my way of showing respect for my mother, but in my heart, I knew I was avoiding the life, and death, unfolding beyond the kitchen.

A day of listening to "At least her suffering is over" and "She was brave to the very end" nearly crushed me. When the funeral procession set off from our house, I was more than grateful that we followed the coffin in our cars instead of on foot. I was shaky with exhaustion and empty of emotion, unable to support my father when we climbed out of the car and entered the cemetery. But he had no one else and clung to my arm, so I couldn't have moved away even if I'd wanted to.

Throughout the entire funeral, I tried but failed to remember my mother as she had been when I last saw her alive. My father was leaning on me more and more heavily. At one point, his knees buckled and I held him up, praying we wouldn't both topple. An unknown man stepped forwards and took hold of my father's other arm.

Afterwards, my father and I were alone, the

neighbours and acquaintances dispersing during the long afternoon, with no one but me left to carry the burden when night came.

The house had become such a miserable place. It was filled with more death than life. Even though the following days were bleak, I felt compelled to stay and take care of my father. Not that he appreciated it. He withdrew into himself, and on those rare occasions he chose to communicate with me, it was with unintelligible sounds, mumbling, and grunting. I didn't recognise him as the person I'd shared the house with for two decades. I kept my nerves at bay by cooking and baking until his freezer and pantry were full.

On the way to the airport two weeks later, I was still torn between relief at going away again and worry over leaving him alone. I told myself it was already too late for so many things that one more failure wouldn't matter.

I returned to Stockholm empty and discouraged. Ståle wanted me to talk about my grief, but I refused. After a while, he stopped trying. But when he suggested I go with his sister to a cookery class to keep myself busy, I indulged him. Unexpectedly, I liked the experience, so I stayed.

The cookery instructor said that she would not simply teach us, she would prompt and motivate us to reveal our talents and inspiration. To her, cooking didn't involve just techniques and skills but also creativity and soul. Her poetic and hopeful words made cooking sound like something I could get lost in, just like when I was a child. The illusion was over when one day Mariane asked me to introduce the class to traditional Slovenian fare.

"But no one likes vegetable stews and potatoes done every which way, and sauerkraut and sausages," I argued.

"I don't remember the recipes, anyway. I won't be able to find the proper ingredients here."

None of my excuses convinced Mariane.

Thinking about what to cook for my classmates kept me awake that night. I thought of the kitchen at home, the laminated worktops and wall units with squeaky doors. The night air was thick with memories and past struggles. I couldn't bear it.

I arrived sluggish and irritable at the school the next morning. Deciding on a dish had drained me as if it were a far more important decision than it was. In the end, I preferred to face Mariane's disappointment than struggle with the thought of using one of my mother's recipes. I made pasta *alla carbonara* instead.

I couldn't face tackling my mother's recipes. The memories they awoke were too painful so soon after her funeral. The food I chose to cook seemed frivolous in comparison, untainted by personal connection. At the school and sometimes at home, I explored the new Nordic diet, fusion cuisine, French dishes—anything distant enough from my past and home. Although Mariane protested, I wouldn't be swayed.

The acute ache following my mother's funeral eased with time but the sadness didn't quite pass. I realised that during my five years abroad I had harboured the hope I would always have a home to return to. I hadn't really worked out what I would do once I was there, but the thought at the back of my mind acted as a safety net. Plan B. Now that my mother was gone, that was no longer true.

I was beginning to lose my second home, too, because no matter how hard I tried to ignore the cracks in my relationship with Ståle, they were getting wider with each month. Once we decided to go our separate ways, the tension weighing on me disappeared and I could think more clearly about what I wanted from life and what to do next. That's how I met Yves—at a cookery school in Paris.

That first day, I was a jumble of nerves. Because of the number of people in the cookery school reception area, the silence was unexpected and it exposed all our insecurities. We stood in small clusters or alone, putting as much distance between each other as possible as if our foreignness was contagious. It was difficult to determine where everyone was from because almost no one spoke, except for the couple closest to me. They half whispered and their words sounded Slavic, but I couldn't hear what they were saying. I guessed they were Polish. Opposite me was a dark-haired, olive-skinned woman, maybe Italian or Spanish. A man, who seemed only slightly older than me, greeted us in English with a German accent. There was a Japanese girl and a girl I was willing to bet was French, but the rest were a mystery. It surprised me almost half of the group were women because I couldn't remember the last time I had seen a female celebrity chef on TV.

It turned out I was right about the French girl. Maybe it was the familiar territory or the language which made her more self-assured and resourceful than the rest of us, but I was grateful when she helped me find my way to the locker room, where we put on our new uniforms. I felt as though I was being initiated into a secret cult. The feeling was both exciting and daunting.

Still, on that first day at the cookery school I was full of dread when the instructor entered the classroom and everyone fell silent.

"Welcome to our school, *Mesdames et Messieurs*," he said, his eyes dark and sharp as he scanned our faces. "I am Yves Amirault and I will be one of your instructors. Prepare to work hard. Work in the kitchen is not for the faint-hearted, wannabe food bloggers, or housewives who think they can upgrade to professional chefs." His eyes fell on me, and while I was none of those, I shrank under his stare.

Although his stylish white chef's uniform with blue trim demanded respect, his scowl and condescending demeanour made me doubt his expertise. The only people who had to resort to arrogance were those lacking in knowledge, I thought.

After another five minutes of warnings about the demands of his profession, he ordered us to follow him to the outdoor market to pick the ingredients for the day's dishes.

As we observed him pick the produce at a stall, choosing, discarding, disparaging vegetables that weren't perfect, the brunette who had helped me decipher my timetable earlier, and whose name I had forgotten, leaned closer and whispered, "His surname fits him perfectly."

I had no idea what his surname meant, so she explained, "Amirault means admiral. He behaves like one, too." She grinned. I snorted with laughter.

The instructor turned to me. "You, what's your name?" His English was barely accented and this only added to my dislike of him.

"Nina," I stammered.

"Last name?" he corrected. Students were called by their surnames. Embarrassment warmed my cheeks. "Švagelj."

He wrinkled his nose, shot me another rude look, and turned away.

Hoping to find an ally in the brunette, I looked at her and shrugged. The girl offered a thin smile in response as if trying to distance herself from me. Her name was Audrey, I remembered.

Despite the inauspicious start, the rest of the day was better. I could easily follow the lessons because they were presented in English. Taking notes and observing the preparation kept me busy enough to avoid paying attention to Amirault.

After the lunch break, we were required to reproduce the dish he had shown us in the morning. Out of the corner of my eye, I followed him as he circled the room, commenting on other students' work, reprimanding them on their cutting technique or the result. I was confident that when he saw my diced onion, I would repair his impression from that morning.

One station away, he grabbed the Brazilian girl's hand and readjusted her fingers into a proper claw grip. Her lips trembled when she nodded at his instructions. Dismissing her, he moved on to me.

He peered over my shoulder and I tensed. I was certain he couldn't find fault with my knife skills. I'd mastered them in the cookery class in Stockholm. Although I promised myself not to acknowledge his presence, when he didn't say a word, I looked at him over my shoulder. He gave me a long, dark look. I felt just as chastised as if he'd yelled at me.

Marvelling at how expressive the instructor could be without using words, I forgot to lower the heat when sautéing the onion. The carefully diced cubes turned brown beyond repair.

"What is this?" I jumped at his voice. I hadn't seen him approach. He raised his eyebrow. There was nothing I could say to justify my mistake. "Managing the temperature is something so simple and basic a child would know how to do it, Nina. Why are you here?" he demanded.

"Excuse me?"

"Start over," he said, and moved on to the next student.

My eyes became moist. I told myself they were onion tears.

By the end of the first week, I hated the fact that most instructors called me by my first name. Apparently, all the other students had more easily pronounceable surnames.

Time passed quickly and soon it was mid-September. The leaves in Luxembourg Gardens began to change and I couldn't get enough of their rich autumnal colours. On a lonely Sunday when I didn't know what to do with myself in this new city, I carried my lunch of spring rolls and a bottle of water to the park. The people passing by all seemed to be going somewhere; there was purpose in their gait.

I used to think I had a goal, too—leave my home village behind and find happiness. It wasn't until my mother died and my relationship failed that I realised I had been wrong. The sadness and disappointment made me grow up. The good things in life gave us purpose, but misery and grief motivated us to grow out of ourselves and into the world. I believed that was what had brought me to Paris.

I saw out of the corner of my eye someone approaching and sitting at the other end. Why on earth couldn't he choose one of the other empty benches along the promenade?

"Hello, Nina," said a voice I recognised.

I turned to look at the man. "Professor?" That I should run into my teacher in a city of two million inhabitants seemed a special sort of bad luck.

"Yves, *s'il te plaît*." His lips twitched as if he was amused by my shock when I gaped. "Recharging your batteries before a new week?"

When he spoke about general things, his English was barely accented. Only when using gastronomy terms, which mostly originated from the French language, anyhow, did his accent become more pronounced. A linguistic irony.

I couldn't believe how shamelessly his brown eyes dropped to my chest and then measured the length of my legs.

"Why does everyone call me by my first name?" I asked, trying to swallow my irritation and divert his attention from my appearance. The question sounded silly once voiced, but it irked me I was being singled out even in such a mixed group as my international class.

"Your surname is unpronounceable."

"It's no more difficult than Velazquez or Cherny," I countered, naming two classmates with whom I had spent a few breaks in the school's winter garden in the past few weeks.

He shrugged and opened a paper bag. I watched as he revealed a cinnamon roll. Its smell reminded me of autumn back home and the tall linden tree by the house gradually, almost absent-mindedly, changing colour. As a teenager I had watched it through the kitchen window and daydreamed of going places, but then someone would always walk into the kitchen and interrupt my dreams.

"Fresh this morning," he said.

At the risk of him rebuking me, I asked, "Bought it or baked it?"

He gave me a look and then bit into the pastry with relish.

I had never seen Ståle or my father or any other man enjoy food in such a way. So instinctively and primitively. So deeply.

Pausing, he lowered the roll and pulled it apart with his fingers. "Here." He offered me a piece. "*Allez*, try it. It's good."

I hesitated then took a tiny bite, barely enough to taste. It wasn't just good. I had eaten *kanelbullar* in Stockholm on a daily basis, so I recognised the spicy, tooth-achingly sweet taste. But Yves's pastry melted in my mouth like mist, something alcoholic giving it an aftertaste that stayed on my tongue long after I had swallowed. "It's delicious," I said.

"Of course."

He was the most arrogant person I had ever had the misfortune of meeting. But after a few weeks at the school, I had discovered he was so good at what he did, I was unable to resent the arrogance. While most people would come off as rude, he was amusing, in a way. During classes, his words so often dripped with sarcasm, I imagined he would bleed it if cut. I suspected if an occasion presented itself, however, he would be more than capable of laughing at himself.

"Of course," I repeated, and couldn't stop myself from smiling.

Not acknowledging my jibe, he said out of the blue, "It's because you remind me of Ninotchka." He finished the roll without offering me another bite. "That's why I call you by your first name. The others just followed suit."

"Ninotchka?"

"The film? Greta Garbo?" He raised his eyebrows when I expressed my ignorance with a shrug.

"I don't know the film, just the actress. She was Swedish. I used to live in Sweden," I clarified after a moment.

"Another thing you two have in common, then."

"What else is there?"

"You have her cheekbones and eyes. Your name. But your uneven teeth spoil the whole effect."

"Thanks. I think." The compliment, regardless of how ambiguous it was, was unexpected. If only he were that willing to praise me in the classroom.

As if reading my mind, he said, "That can't and won't make up for your lack of skill."

"Wouldn't think of it," I said, but on the tail end of my sarcastic words came a feeling of thankfulness. I wouldn't want him giving me an advantage over the others; I would lose all respect for him as a teacher if he did that.

"I will leave you to it, then. *Au revoir*." He stood, dusting the crumbs from his black trousers, his long, tattooed fingers making the gesture elegant.

I didn't feel comfortable enough using French, so I said, "I'll see you tomorrow."

As he walked away, I felt his departure as strongly as if a large cloud had dissipated and let the sun shine through. The feeling was pleasant, but the change stark.

"*En fait*, I prefer your lips to Garbo's."

My head jerked up, hearing his voice, so unexpectedly close and which was somewhere between flattering and mocking. But he turned again before I could catch his eye.

At the end of November, when I thought back and realised how much I had learned, I wondered how it was possible I had only been attending the course for three months. On my lunch breaks, I shared coffee and snacks with classmates, and in the evenings, I explored the streets of Paris. That was more or less my only free time. I was quite content that school kept me busy, and spent most of my time in the kitchen, either at the school or home.

I enjoyed the classes and devoured my lessons. Amirault still picked on me in class, but I no longer feared him. He had no reason to be meaner to me than to the others but I didn't resent it because there were moments that made it worthwhile, moments when he reluctantly praised my work in front of everyone. Then again, there were other moments.

"Not like that," he said as he passed behind me one Friday afternoon. It had been a long, cold week on the brink of winter, and I couldn't wait to escape the school building and enjoy the quiet and cosiness of my apartment.

I turned to look at him to see what exactly he was criticising. He had said before that my cutting technique was fine. I couldn't understand the sudden change: I was dicing vegetables the same way as always.

He glanced at me with a hint of amusement. He caught me between the worksurface and his tall frame. The sensations zapping through my body were disturbing because they were a perplexing mix of nerves and interest.

What was he doing?

His right hand took hold of mine on the knife. "Like this," he said, first pressing the point down and then the rest of the blade. The leeks crunched and oozed juice on the cutting board. "Like this." He repeated the move. And again. His dexterity amazed me because he was left-handed and yet he guided me with his right hand on the knife with precision and confidence.

His firm grip warmed my hand. Beads of sweat formed under my armpits and between my breasts. It was pretence. I understood now that my technique was adequate. His, however, could have been subtler. I smiled. He caught it and acknowledged it with an amused look.

"Perhaps you could cook a Slovenian dish for us sometime," he said out of the blue, taking a step back and releasing me from his embrace.

I stammered before I gathered my wits. "I'd rather not." I would be lying if I said I hadn't liked his attention earlier, but this was something different altogether. This was just like Sweden. Why did everyone think that cooking the food we grew up with was vital to developing as a chef? I could learn and create without that burden. I intended to prove it to him. Just the thought of recreating one of my mother's dishes… The memories it awakened, the hollow feeling inside; I wasn't ready to tackle that.

He raised an eyebrow.

"Our food is too basic," I said, curtly. "You wouldn't like it."

He opened his mouth to speak, but I turned away.

Two weeks later, I was stood by the shelves, gathering ingredients to prepare mutton, when he passed me. He muttered something I couldn't quite catch.

"Pardon?" I leaned in to hear him. Our faces were inches apart. His lips formed words but they eluded me. His eyes were teasing; he sensed my confusion. He had whispered on purpose, to draw me near. But rather than unsettle me, his attention made me feel surer of myself as I returned to my place at the food preparation area. I was too old to let him embarrass me.

Despite the increasingly complicated personal relationship, I loved to watch him cook. Amirault worked as though cooking was instinctual rather than an acquired skill. The handles of his knives had moulded to his all-knowing hands after years of skilful use. I wondered how that felt, being touched and directed with such sureness, and my skin responded with a warm flush.

Amirault intrigued and frightened me in equal measure. He had an aura I associated with people who were brilliant at what they did. But he could also be brutal to anyone who didn't meet his standards, like many people whose outstanding achievements made them oblivious to everyone else's feelings and aspirations. The worst was when you failed in class and he yelled in French. Sometimes he started out in English, trying to be patient and informative, but he quickly switched to abusive French, doling out expletives as though he were chopping a tomato *concassé*. Being reduced to an uncomprehending idiot doubled the humiliation. Knowledge made him powerful; arrogance made him wield that power most effectively. I awaited his every pass behind my back with trepidation, and every time he yelled and shamed me in front of the class, I was in awe of his tall, wiry frame, which made me feel small. His booming voice, otherwise smooth and rich, jarred like the clank of a pot on the tiled floor. His arms gesticulated as if he were physically trying to cram knowledge and experience into my head. The way his cool indifference exploded into a crackling flame aroused me. To watch someone so powerful and so aware of his power was intoxicating.

The techniques we learned were increasingly complex and demanding. I struggled to spatchcock a chicken, removing its backbone to flatten it and reduce the roasting time. My knife slipped and I looked up to see if Amirault was anywhere near and had perhaps seen my clumsiness. Instead, I found Audrey staring at me.

"What?" I said. Her thoughtful expression made me nervous because I couldn't guess what she had on her mind. I found the French quite reticent, particularly when you didn't speak their language well. Most people I had met in Paris so far only spoke rudimentary English, apart from the professors and other foreigners in my class.

Audrey had helped me with my timetable that first day and we had gone for drinks after lessons a few times. She had even introduced me to some of her friends. But afterwards, the potential friendship had hit a wall with both of us being reserved, waiting for the other to make the next move.

The tray with the chicken caught on the door of the oven and I had to realign it to push it in and close the door. "Is something wrong?" I asked when she didn't say anything.

Amirault had left the classroom, and I saw him go down the hallway and into our break room.

"*Non*," Audrey said, wiping the worksurface with a rag, not looking at me.

Her frown and eyes, which kept darting to me, suggested otherwise. She gave in at last and looked up. "You're playing with fire, Nina," she said, gesturing down the hall with her head.

"I don't know what you mean."

She watched me. Then, when I didn't offer anything more, she shrugged. "Make sure you won't be putting the fire out with tears, *Ninotchka*."

She must have heard Amirault using his nickname for me that morning. I knew I was being foolish and naïve but I was proud that people saw how important I was to him.

SIX

The smell of the *potimarron* crescents as I tipped them from the oven tray into a bowl reminded me of roasted chestnuts from my childhood, and my mouth watered. It was usually food that brought back old memories, but lately I'd been so busy with school I didn't have time to think about home. I was grateful for that.

I crumbled blue cheese on top of the squash and tossed the ingredients to mix them. Taking a fork out of the drawer, I went to sit and eat on the sofa bed. I had unfolded the pull-out bed the day I moved in three months before and it had stayed that way.

Leaning back, I had just bitten into a piece of the squash when someone knocked on the door. The previous week, I'd lent my bicycle pump to my downstairs neighbour. She must have brought it back.

But when I opened the door, my eyes fell on Yves Amirault. The bottle of wine in his hand was almost as dark as his black shirt.

"I was nearby and thought I'd come see if you've settled in," he said with a sure, smooth voice. But his intense stare betrayed his uncertainty.

I opened the door wider, and he walked in. In silence, he poured the Côtes-du-Rhône into the two glasses I put on the table. How many of his female students had he visited like this?

He glanced around the studio apartment; his face gave nothing away. I imagined he lived in a trendy place, exuding minimalism and timeless bachelor elegance. But I wasn't certain he was a bachelor.

"Please, sit," I said, motioning to the table.

He ignored my words and took a piece of the *potimarron*, eating it standing up. "Simple and tasteful," he said, and took another bite.

"*Les délices de l'automne*," I said, remembering a slogan I'd seen in a shop window on my way home earlier that day.

"You should learn French. You pronounce it well."

I wasn't sure if he meant it or was teasing me. "I still struggle with English. I don't need another language to complicate things."

He munched on another reddish-brown crescent. Every now and then, he closed his eyes as if taking a moment to savour the taste.

"Your English is excellent," I said.

"I grew up in New York."

That was not an answer I expected. I waited for an explanation, but when he didn't offer one, I asked, "When did you move to Paris?"

He lifted his eyes up from the bowl. "I was born here, but we moved to the States for six years when I was three."

That was why his English was fluent and almost unaccented. Most Frenchmen I'd encountered either didn't want to speak English or they struggled with it even more than I did.

He stepped to the large white-framed window, turning

his back to me. I recognised that as a sign he didn't want to talk about his past. I knew so little about him that it was surprising how right him being in my apartment felt. He turned to me, and even his penetrating eyes seemed to be asking me what I was doing. I had never before been so aware of my body. Blood pounded in the veins in my wrists and behind my ears. The smell of his soap filled my nostrils.

He stood in front of me although I hadn't noticed him take the few steps there. The thin lines around his eyes looked delicate compared to his callused hands and tattooed arms and fingers.

His hand brushed my arm as he picked up an oil-soaked sage leaf from the bowl on the table behind me. He inhaled its smell and closed his eyes. "Don't you find the aroma of sage arousing?"

I didn't know where to look or what to say.

"You're a complicated woman, Ninotchka."

Was I? And how could he tell?

"It's in the way you look at me, weighing the pros and cons."

More than weighing pros and cons, I was confused. But when his warm fingers circled my wrist, and a little tremor went through my body, I knew why I hadn't demanded he leave. His self-confidence and dominance attracted me. I wanted a taste of it.

"I'm breaking the rules," he said. "So let's keep this between us, shall we?"

It was at the very least unethical to have a relationship with an instructor. To hide my nerves, I took a sip from my glass, mirroring Yves. The wine went down smoothly, and a moment later, I tasted its spice on his tongue.

The sex was consuming and quick. Afterwards, his deep, hot breath warmed my skin. Our arms were entwined, legs touching. My body hummed while my mind was somehow numb and painfully alert at the same time.

The strap of my bra dug into my back and my skirt was bunched around my waist. The rest of the clothes were scattered across the hardwood floor. I didn't know whether to get dressed or undress the rest of the way. Would he stay or get up and leave?

I itched with the need to say something to break the silence but I was unsure how he would react. Would there be a repeat of this?

He slid onto his feet, not bothering to cover his nakedness. The five o'clock sun bronzed his shoulders as he stretched in front of the window. His pale skin was in deep contrast to the black ink of his tattoos and dark hair. I cringed at the thought a neighbour might spot him while enjoying her *cafe gourmand* across the alley.

He dressed, pulling up his black trousers, belting them, tucking the black shirt in smoothly, mechanically. His profile was all hooded eyes and straight nose. His rough stubble was imprinted on my neck and thighs, burning like paprika. In the fading light, his pursed lips looked severe. I had yet to see him give a genuine smile.

"I'll see you tomorrow," I said when he kissed me. My insecurity made the words sound like a question.

"Don't expect any privileges," he said.

His clipped tone hurt my pride. Then I saw the glint in his eyes. I would be too generous if I called it a smile; it was more a spark of amusement.

"Of course not."

On his way out, he stopped at the small whiteboard by the door. Picking up the pen on a lanyard, he wrote something in the upper right corner. "*À bientôt*," he said over his shoulder.

I sighed once he was gone, then got up to read his message. The ten digits he'd written suggested this wasn't a one-time thing. I wasn't sure how I felt about that.

Yves's authoritativeness, brilliance, and arrogance pulled me in like a black hole. My feelings for him weren't delicate or gentle; it was a power struggle: with him, with myself. Something that thrilled me and made me dislike myself at the same time. I had struggled with these feelings since the beginning of our relationship. There was a bone-deep attraction I couldn't understand, much less justify. He didn't buy me gifts or make me feel special. Yet I hungered for his honest opinions, the passion with which he imbued his every action, his simple lovemaking, which I could only describe as earthy and real, more physical than anything I had known, and yet, maybe because of that, sublime. It was difficult to imagine anyone ever replacing Yves in my life. But I knew there would be others. Yves would not stay. Or maybe I wouldn't. We had both entered this relationship with too much selfishness for it to have any hope of permanence.

Over the following months, pretending in front of classmates became difficult as Yves and I met often. We learned each other's bodies like new languages, as if that could substitute for the lack of meaningful conversation.

One night, after a disastrous day at the cookery school Yves arrived late from his restaurant. He barely greeted me before he leaned in and kissed me, open-mouthed, hands on my waist, then my breasts.

"Sorry, I'm not in the mood," I managed between kisses.

"What's wrong?" he asked but kept nibbling at my ear.

"Nothing." It wasn't true but I couldn't find words to explain. "A bad day." The end of the course was approaching and I was concerned about how I would do at the exams. I worried the other instructors suspected I had a relationship with Yves and that it might affect my final assessment. But he'd wave it off if I told him about my concerns.

"Ah, you're nervous about the exams."

"Well, that's normal." I was defensive because his perceptiveness caught me off guard.

He scoffed and stepped back. "Your inferiority complex doesn't help either."

"What are you talking about?"

"Don't pretend you don't know. You keep making excuses, saying how you're not good enough, how you don't deserve this or that. It's annoying."

"I'm honest. I don't want to be pretentious." I was tempted to add "Like you", but it would serve no purpose other than to escalate the quarrel. What were we doing, anyway? Fighting about such a trivial thing as pre-exam nerves. But that was how we both were: defensive and aggressive the moment we felt vulnerable and helpless. The smallest sign of trouble and we had our guard up.

Yves moved further away, looking out through the window. The glass was framed by a ring of condensation from the mugginess of my studio. "Not pretentious. Realistic. That's what you need to be. Look at the world and see it as it is," he said without glancing at me.

"But I can only see it through my eyes," I argued.

A sad smile curved his lips, which was so unlike him I wondered what was going through his mind. What was it he wasn't telling me?

"Your eyes are fine," he said, as he returned to me. He tapped my temple with his finger. "It's in here that you need to fix things. You know that. I know you know it, because you're one of the smartest people I know."

I raised my eyebrows. He rarely praised anyone even when praise was due. His words made me soften towards him in spite of his earlier accusations.

"Shit happens, Nina. You learn the lesson and move on. You don't let it chain you to a place. Or a time, or a person," he added after a moment.

His hair was dishevelled from my fingers. I wished I could turn back time to the moments before this discussion. Things seemed easier when we didn't talk.

"You don't know what it's like." I wanted him to understand but I couldn't tell him about my parents, about feeling unwanted by my own family. I was too ashamed of it. Reluctantly, I added, "You don't know anything about where I come from."

He let out a deep sigh. "So you didn't have a happy childhood. Who did, anyway? But you can't let that dictate the rest of you." He sank his fingers into my hair. "A good chef finds her inspiration in who she is. Who are you, Ninotchka, if you refuse to cook your favourite childhood food? If you're set on adopting every fucking cuisine but your own?" He leaned into me then, and my entire body vibrated with a deep sigh, such was his power over me. "Don't let the past restrict you. Use it to your advantage. Let go, move on," he murmured.

His eyes, dark pools of self-centredness, stared me down. I relaxed into him, willing him to shut up and hug me. I pressed my nose into his neck and inhaled the smell of his warm skin.

"Just like you let me fuck you," he said, "and then you get out of bed and go on living like nothing happened. Treat life the same way." There was some perverted satisfaction in his voice, as if he was deliberately trying to hurt me.

I didn't plan to slap him. It came as much of a surprise to me as to him.

He jerked back. "What was that for?"

I stalked to the window and he followed, stopping behind me, not touching, but I could feel his heat imprint on my back. There was less cockiness in him when he said, "You'll start your internship soon. You'll snap like a twig. Take a day or two, or a week, and sort things out in your head. Woman up. And then call me."

"And you'll come fuck me?" I sounded strangled. Only a thread of hopefulness separated me from hating him. How would that make him feel if he knew? Would he even care?

"You'll beg me for it," he said in my ear, and washed the hate away in a shiver down my spine until it pooled at my feet. "Because you know I'm right. Because you need me to call your bluff. And because I can give you more pleasure than you thought possible."

His crude words made me feel naked. But he was right, I would beg him and I would love it. He got under my skin because he knew me; he understood the way my mind worked. He was like a beacon, showing me the way. I was becoming too reliant on him. But I wasn't sure I had the strength or the will to break the ties.

To avoid facing Yves's reflection in the window I closed my eyes. When I opened them again, I saw him rub his cheek on his way to the door. I whispered, "I could hate you. So easily."

I could imagine his wry smile. Then it struck me that my words were a lie. Did he know?

After starting my internship at Yves's restaurant Pomme d'Amour, I progressed slowly through the ranks. Since finishing school as second best in my year, I had started at the *garde manger* station where I worked on appetisers and amuse-bouches. Then I moved up to an *entremetière*, cooking side dishes and vegetables. I had struggled for a while until I became familiar with the intense rhythm of the station. Tonight was my first night as a *poissonnière*. It was my chance to prove myself and earn my place in this kitchen.

Mise en place was going well until someone salted the already seasoned salmon fillets. When I realised the mistake, I shouted for two aides to help me fix it, but now we were all behind schedule.

Yves stayed in the background. I caught him glancing at me a few times. He looked serious, but not yet worried. I told myself that was a sign I shouldn't be worried either. But while there wasn't a trace of perspiration on Yves, rivulets of sweat rolled down my back and my hands shook.

At six, the orders started coming. The tickets became a blur that I thought would make me faint. I hurried with the salmon and barked at an assistant to be careful with the sauce when it started bubbling around the edges of the pan.

The baking tin I was getting out of the oven caught on the door and I toppled half of its contents on the floor. My hands were shaking to the point of being unable to hold things. I had a dreadful feeling I would start crying any minute.

I needed Yves's help and support, but I heard him calling out to someone further off in the kitchen. I didn't even know where he was or who he was calling, and I was supposed to know everything that was going on in the kitchen at any given moment. It was vital to be aware of it all and to stay composed, to know where each and every aide was working, to lead them and give out orders. I was losing control of the situation. I would fail. The realisation was sudden and sharp. After everything I had invested in this, I would flunk this one final test.

I bumped into someone standing behind me. "Move," I bit out, steam getting in my eyes.

"Yves sent me to take over," Thoma said. "He needs you in the storeroom."

"Now?" The idea of leaving my post during rush hour was insane.

"He insisted."

I glanced around the kitchen and the chaos. The main dish stations were in the centre of the kitchen, and the other chefs were at the workstations along the two longest sides. The storeroom door was on the right, tucked into the corner off the side-dish station.

If I was gone for a minute, things couldn't get much worse. I closed my eyes briefly and hoped a miracle would happen in the meantime.

The chill and darkness of the storeroom were a shock

for my overheated body. I swatted the switch and the initial blinking of the neon lights was as unsure as I felt. I wiped my forehead and pinched the bridge of my nose, trying to stop the headache brewing behind my eyes. The smell of food that was stored on the shelves all around me nauseated me. I'd had enough. I just wanted to go outside, breathe in some fresh air, and go far, far away from the kitchen.

I heard Yves stride in. Before I could react, he grabbed my shoulders and turned me to face him. I wished he would hug me and tell me everything would be all right. I wanted his comforting smell and his warm voice to console me. For once, I wished he would just be my lover, not my boss and mentor.

"Get a grip, woman," he said. I opened my mouth to say I needed a word of encouragement not him yelling at me, but he wouldn't even let me speak.

"One thing at a time, like we taught you. Clean station, discipline, and no panic. Give orders to your aides and then trust them to fulfil them. And first and foremost, calm the fuck down. You're running around like a headless chicken. You've been doing well for the past six months. Tonight is no different."

Tears welled in my eyes. I knew he wasn't chastising me but stating facts, but I was exhausted. I couldn't do this. I would never enter a restaurant kitchen again. I would go work in a sock factory or something. I hadn't wanted to be a chef; I started on this path by chance.

Yves's warm, rough-skinned hands moved from the crunching grip on my shoulders to my clammy cheeks. He leaned in, and I thought he would kiss my mouth. He pressed his lips to my forehead instead. He whispered, "I know your passion, Ninotchka. If you get it together and do this, you'll never regret it. You'll be hooked for life."

His voice was so intimate I could feel the words rather than just hear them. The deep calm in him and my desire to prove myself to him as the ultimate authority had a surprising effect on me. I wanted him to kiss me, to tear off my clothes, and let me feel his pale, tired skin. I wanted him with a hunger I only otherwise felt for food.

I nodded. My throat was too tight to thank him. If I survived tonight, there would be plenty of time.

"Go out and rule the kingdom," he said behind my back as I walked out. I realised it wasn't because he had power over me that I put up with him but because his skillset was the benchmark I wanted to reach. Exceed. I needed him close to compare myself to him. I just needed him close.

Rounding the grease-spattered hobs, it occurred to me he might know me better than I knew myself. He didn't tell me everything would be all right or that I could do it. Instead, he gave me a reason to try to do my best. He dangled a juicy organic carrot in front of my nose—the satisfaction I would get out of conquering my fears. Manipulative bastard.

Through the fog of hurried, hard work, I caught glimpses of him throughout the evening. He was there, doing his work, not interfering. Thoma was my right hand. He was the most efficient and precise cook I had seen, despite his size and chunky fingers. My control on things slipped two more times but I recovered and brought the evening to a successful finish at ten o'clock. Cleaning up and mise en place for the next day followed and it was four in the morning by the time I fell into bed, clothes on and kitchen grease in my hair.

I got my wits together for a late lunch the next day. Braising a steak, I thought of how all that umami was hidden beneath the frosty crystals of the frozen meat. No one could guess at its delicious taste with a crystallised, misty surface like that. Just like Yves—an unyielding crust over a rich, sumptuous core. He slapped you with his left hand and afterwards caressed with his right where it stung most.

God forbid Yves found out I had used frozen meat instead of a fresh steak. I only managed a few bites anyway. The taste and smell of food from last night was still too strong on my tongue and nose. The salad was easier to eat. I pottered around the flat. I was thinking about calling Audrey for a coffee at Angelina's when Yves showed up.

He kissed me, kicking the door closed behind his back. We made slow, tender love. My muscles still hurt from all the tension the night before, and he massaged them until they loosened up. I lay boneless, overflowing with a heavy, but not unpleasant exhaustion for the second time in the last twelve hours. I didn't move when he clambered out of bed.

"What are you looking for?" I asked when he rummaged through the two cupboards that comprised my kitchen. On top of one stood the cooker, and the sink was squeezed in between that and the window.

"The kettle?"

"You know I don't own one. I don't drink tea," I said. I didn't even have to speak up as there were just three long strides separating the kitchen area from the sofa bed. The column in between created an illusion of privacy. I'd have been more diligent in putting the bed away every day had I entertained more often, but as Yves was more or less my only visitor, privacy didn't matter.

"It's a special tea. It'll restore your energy." He filled a pot with water and put it on the two-ring cooker.

"It was hell. I don't want to ever experience it again." I knew tomorrow night would be the same, and then the night after, and the night after that.

"Nonsense," he said. Two biscuits tumbled across the worktop when he tore the box open with too much force.

"It was," I insisted.

"You did great. I've seen others leave before service started."

"No! Really? Why didn't you tell me last night? I thought I was a failure. I thought…"

He shrugged. "There was no need. I knew you'd make it."

"How? I didn't."

He poured the steaming water into two mugs. He returned the pot to the worktop and picked up the tray, bringing it to the bed. The heady smell of the steeping tea made me drowsy.

"You've got passion. When you decide to do something, you carry it through."

"I almost decided to go work in a sock factory last night."

He frowned, but I didn't elaborate.

He blew on his tea, and for a moment, the steam made his face look hazy. "You didn't make a decision last night. You made it that first day on the steps of the school. You were a knot of nerves. But you persisted."

"You saw me?" I thought back to the first day. It baffled me that I hadn't seen him before he entered the classroom. He was not the sort of man one could miss. I must really have been nervous.

"Of course. You were a vision. Your cheeks were pink from anxiety, you were biting your lip. You almost tripped picking up the notebook you dropped on the steps." If I hadn't known him, I'd have thought he was nostalgic.

"And still you tortured me in class that day."

He grinned. "I wanted to see how determined you were."

"So?"

"You're here, aren't you?"

"I could still change my mind."

"No, you couldn't," he said with conviction.

I sighed, frustrated. I could. But I wouldn't.

He stared out the window of my studio one evening as the outlines of the Paris roofs were turning a bluish tone. "*Entre chien et loup*," he said.

I understood the words *chien* and *loup* but I couldn't fathom how they had anything to do with the scene in front of him.

"It means it's getting so dark you can't tell a dog from a wolf. It also means the fine line between the familiar and the alien, the dangerous," he clarified, and turned to look at me. One half of his face was bathed in the light from the bedside lamp, the other reflected the dark outside the window. He was describing himself, I thought.

"Which one are you?" I asked.

He flashed me a grin, his white teeth glinting.

He joined me on the bed and our bodies stopped

caring about who was wolf, who was dog, who was prey. There were moments I didn't know where my body ended and his began. His hands urged me to roll onto my belly, interrupting me mid-sigh. My snarl of frustration deepened and stretched to a loud climax minutes later.

"*Dieu*, I needed that," Yves panted, and rolled off me onto his back.

"Hard day?" My tongue felt sluggish.

"Week. I had to sack a sous-chef at Vermillon. He was bringing chaos into the team."

The unhappiness in his voice prompted me to turn to him. "You're not happy with that?"

"He had potential. Very creative. Great mind. But he was too stubborn and volatile." He gesticulated wildly with his hands.

Too much like you, I thought. "You care about your employees."

"I care about *a lot* of people." His voice was snappy as if I had intimated that he didn't.

Instead of calming him, as I knew I should, I asked, "Like who?"

"Family, for one."

"You have brothers and sisters?" He once told me his father had died a long time ago and he'd mentioned his mother once or twice, but there had been no talk of siblings.

"Three sisters." His tone was calmer now.

"No!" I had imagined him an only son, used to getting everything he wanted and having everyone's undivided attention. There was no other way, in my mind, for him to become so arrogant and domineering, and rude. Now I found out he had three sisters. How could that be? I wasn't usually so wrong about people.

"Anouk, Edwige, Marion. Two older, one younger," he said.

"Are you close?" I asked. I couldn't believe he hadn't told me about his sisters. Disappointment and hurt formed a knot in my throat.

"*Oui.*"

I sat up. It puzzled me that I had been in a relationship with a man for a year and a half and didn't know the first thing about his family. Was it my fault? Was I blind, indifferent, asocial? Or wasn't I important enough for him to want me to know his loved ones?

"You never asked," he said, as if reading my mind.

When I had been most vulnerable, I told him things I hadn't told anyone. I told him about how I had never felt wanted by my parents, about the strange silences, and all that tension between us. I told him how I left it all behind because I couldn't cope with it. "But I told you about my family and you didn't bother mentioning you have three sisters you're close to?"

"Don't get upset over nothing, Ninotchka. You wouldn't want to meet them."

I spread my arms in incomprehension. How on earth could he know that? "They're fussy and chatty. Prying."

"Why would you assume I wouldn't like friendly, chatty women?"

He frowned. "You're, well, with me."

I bristled. "But I am not you, Yves. I am not haughty and condescending. Who says I wouldn't like other people's company? Perhaps I'd like to go out sometimes instead of you coming here where we just eat, fuck, and then you leave."

Perhaps not everything I said was true, particularly about wanting other people's company, but I was still outraged. I flung myself out of bed. I searched for my pants in the sheets, and pulled them up my legs. "You're selfish, Yves. And self-absorbed."

I pulled the black t-shirt over my head. The smell of his deodorant washed over me and I realised my mistake. I made to take it off, but he stopped me. "It looks good on you. Keep it."

He walked up to me, holding me to him and leaning his chin on my bowed head. "I don't think about these things, Nina. They fly over my head. For fourteen hours a day, I focus on food. That's my everyday. I don't deliberately keep you in the dark."

"I don't believe you."

"It's the truth."

His tone was pleading, but I wondered about other things he hadn't told me. Was it because for him I didn't exist outside my bed or his kitchen? He probably had a separate life out there on the Paris streets, a life I wasn't part of.

I shrugged out of his hug and moved away. I pulled up my trousers. I combed my hair off my face with my fingers, scanning the flat for a hairband. "I've got things to do."

"Nina?"

I gathered his clothes and pushed them into his hands. "I'll call you when I have time."

"Are you kicking me out?" The disbelief on his face was almost comical.

"Oh." I lifted the hem of the black t-shirt and pulled it off. "Here."

Yves took it without protest this time. He still had a disbelieving half-smile on his face. I ignored him as I searched for my own shirt to cover my breasts.

"Nina. Ninotchka."

"I'll call." I was more tired and less resolute than I sounded.

He pulled on his shirt but stumbled over the buttons. Belting his trousers, he left the shirt half untucked.

"Fine," he said through gritted teeth, and left.

I closed the door and didn't feel a shred of regret.

After eight months, I began to feel at home in the restaurant kitchen. I had familiarised myself with every scratch on the stainless steel surfaces, with how there was little space at the side-dish station, how the two chefs on the mains had to work in a choreographed dance not to bump into each other, how my locker door jammed and the door to Yves's office squeaked. When you spend ten or twelve hours in the same space day after day, it becomes a part of you, you breathe it, dream it—you either grow to love it or hate it. Some days, when everything went wrong and my work was not up to scratch, I hated it. But it was becoming clear I could not live without it. I could lose myself in cooking. During the long hours I spent in the kitchen, my problems vanished; memories of my mother and the fact I hadn't called home in months receded to the back of my mind. Cooking freed me. It was an escape. So it was easier to understand Yves and what he saw in this business and why he was the way he was.

Sometime during the first months of cookery school, he had quoted someone saying that cooking was like love; you either entered into it with abandon or not at all. I had thought I understood what he meant, but now that I had experienced it, I knew I hadn't had a clue. I worried there was an exhaustible amount of passion in each person, and if cooking drained it all, there would be nothing left to give to another soul. Out of all the staff in our kitchen, only Uriel, the long-standing dishwasher, and Katie, one of the aides, were in steady relationships. Well, and Yves and me.

But the unwavering dedication each one on the team felt for cooking meant I could rely on them. Working in a restaurant kitchen was a bit like joining the military. You didn't have to like your fellow soldiers as people as long as you could trust them to have your back. I was lucky to be surrounded by people like the generous Thoma, the serious but steadfast Irene, and Yves, who sometimes felt like my mirror image—reversed, but essentially the same.

Most nights, I fell into bed exhausted but also fired up by work well done. Happy clients gave me a satisfaction I had never experienced before. While Yves and I had never been completely in tune with each other, he filled my life with the hope that maybe I had the capacity to feel happy. I suspected the moments when we weren't in synch with each other were caused by our inability to find the right words at the right time. His most passionate and tender moments were in French, as mine were in Slovenian. He raged with *putains* and *merdes*, and he praised me with soft words I didn't understand. Only our indifference seemed to be English. It was perhaps because of this we misunderstood each other so often.

On the morning of Valentine's Day, mise en place started as usual. The holiday was growing in popularity in France, but Yves insisted we should offer the same seasonal dishes as the day before. I would have liked a break from our usual menu, but with the hard work we did every day, I also appreciated that my job was a little bit easier because of routine.

After seasoning the meat, I was wiping down the worksurface when a small bouquet of tulips appeared in front of me. My breath hitched. The gesture made something in me go soft and tender and fill with longing.

"For the best chef around," Thoma said when I turned to face him.

I struggled not to show my disappointment but I must not have been successful. Thoma's chocolate brown eyes glanced at Yves on the other side of the kitchen.

I knew Thoma was not interested in me as a woman. I had seen the way he looked at our *garde manger* chef, Irene, far too often to assume he had feelings for me. But he was a sweet man and such gestures weren't unusual for him.

"Shouldn't these go to someone else?" I said.

"Oh, no, Yves would misunderstand," Thoma said with a serious face and deep voice, then he cracked a wide grin. The traces of his rough youth in the shape of two curved scars across his left cheek made him look far more dangerous than he was.

"I've something better for her," Thoma whispered, and winked, not even trying to pretend he didn't know whom I was talking about.

I laughed. "That's good, then. Thanks for these. They're lovely."

I didn't think Yves had seen the exchange, but when he came by to see how I was doing with preparations, he stayed longer than usual. Someone brought us coffee, and we took a five-minute breather.

"Didn't expect you to be one for celebrating Valentine's," he said.

"I just got a bouquet of flowers, that's all."

I leaned on the worksurface and he sat on a chair next to it. It was a strange arrangement, me looking down at him. I liked it. He appeared more affable like this; more man and less god. I ignored the urge to comb my fingers through his hair, which was the colour of bitter coffee. The image of him sitting down, relaxed, staring up at me, awakened strange feelings. Ones that didn't belong in a kitchen. Or my cautious heart.

"Yes, but you received it for Valentine's Day," he insisted.

I was about to say the flowers should have come from a different man but I bit my tongue. "Yes, I'm clichéd for liking them."

Looking at me, he said, "The whole world is clichéd. If you do the clichéd thing, you're clichéd. If you don't, you're clichéd, too. You know why?"

I was amused by the fervour in his voice. Not knowing where he was going with this, I waited to be enlightened.

"Because we talk too much. There's no mystery. Information from one end of the world reaches the other within nanoseconds. I know everything I want and more about everything and everyone. In 1920, some bloke buys his girl flowers, he's romantic. Now someone uses an aeroplane banner to propose, he succeeds, it goes on YouTube, blog, what have you. The next day a hundred other men do it all around the world and it's already clichéd. We talk too much, we chat online, on the phone, on the radio, we chat on the streets, in private, with kids, and the priest."

Ironically, that was the longest speech I had heard him give outside the classroom.

"Talking is important," I said.

"At the right moment, about the right things."

"Yes, but you can't have a sincere relationship if you don't talk to each other." My mother and father had rarely spoken to one another. They'd used me as the messenger. I had felt used, but in a twisted way also important and needed.

"We're doing fine with little talk," he said, and his hand gravitated to me, wrapping around my wrist. There was something infinitely gentle in this touch, and because I was so unused to gentleness from him, it affected me more than it should.

"Sometimes we are, sometimes we aren't," I said, half holding my breath from the shock of the unusual intimacy in the middle of the kitchen.

"You think we'd be better off talking more?"

I shrugged. "I'd like to know more about you. Sometimes I think I know more about my downstairs neighbour, and I've only spoken to her twice."

"I'm not as deep and complicated as you think." He smiled, oddly self-deprecating. "What you see is pretty much what you get with me."

"I'm not sure I believe you," I murmured, remembering the story about how Yves and Thoma had met.

According to Uriel, Yves had caught Thoma stealing his motorbike when Thoma was just eighteen. In the struggle that followed, Thoma slashed Yves behind his ear with a bowie knife. Thoma was charged with attempted murder and was sentenced to a year in prison once the extenuating circumstances of his terminally ill mother and having to care for a ten-year-old brother were revealed. He was released after six months, with Yves waiting at the entrance with a job offer. Thoma had started as a dishwasher but rose quickly and ambitiously through the ranks.

Or so the story went. I could never get Yves or Thoma to confirm it.

"Words can be misleading," Yves said. "For example, you're letting what I said just now influence you, instead of using your true knowledge of who I am. Because you do know who I am, you just have to let yourself admit it."

I watched him stare at me. He seemed so real and exposed as the fresh sweat wafted off his black t-shirt. The vein on his temple pulsed, and the rough scab of an old cut on his thumb scratched my inner wrist. I did know him. But the shadow of insecurity in his brown eyes that suggested my opinions mattered and his tender, vulnerable expression were a novelty. I had craved to see this side of him, but now that I did, it scared me.

I sighed. The noise of the kitchen was not the right backdrop for such conversations. "I wish we were less complicated. Our minds, I mean."

"If the human brain were simple enough for us to unravel it, then we'd be too stupid to really understand it," he said, an amused grin on his lips.

"I know, but I can wish, can't I?"

"Of course." His empty cup made a scraping noise as he slid it across the steel surface. When he got up and leaned closer, it was so unexpected, inconceivable, I almost pulled away. He kissed me so softly and slowly and my insides twisted into a knot of longing.

The kitchen quieted as the whole place took a collective breath, and then noise started up as work resumed when Yves let go of me. He smiled, wistfully, and returned to his tasks. It took me a while to return to mine.

My year-long internship at the restaurant was drawing to a close and my relationship with Yves was becoming more meaningful and tender. Then Philippe walked in through the staff entrance one day, announcing his presence like a film star.

Philippe's English was a mix of French Rs and Australian accent. He was thickset and had large hands. I liked his friendly laugh but I was careful not to show how I disliked his patronising comments about my dishes. I told myself that they didn't matter; he was Yves's friend, that was all.

During his first week at Pomme d'Amour, I didn't spend much time in his company, or Yves's. The two men had a party of their own, and I wasn't invited. They laughed at crass jokes I only vaguely understood, I heard them bicker over recipes, Philippe told him about his life in Melbourne, and Yves was suggestively silent about his in Paris. From how they reminisced about their joint past, I inferred they had been friends since cookery school, but while Yves stayed in Paris, Philippe had moved down under and opened a bistro in Melbourne fifteen years before. They visited each other regularly, sharing new techniques and recipes, riling each other up, competing.

On his seventh day in Paris, Philippe noticed me. I was finalising one of the mains on a plate just before it was taken out to the dining room, and his scrutiny made me nervous.

"That was perfection," he said.

"Thank you."

After hours, when he was getting ready to leave with Yves, and I was starting to clean the kitchen, he asked, in passing, "Have you ever thought of working somewhere else?"

My internship with Pomme d'Amour and Yves's mentorship would be over in a month, but I supposed I would be kept on as a member of the staff. Philippe's question made me doubt it for the first time. Yves had never actually said I could stay and I had never asked. Perhaps I was assuming too much.

"I haven't really thought about the future yet," I said, ashamed to admit my naivety.

"No?" He observed me with interest in his shrewd blue eyes.

Two days later, he invited me to come and cook for him in Melbourne. "I own a bistro, ingeniously named Philippe's." He chuckled so his red cheeks trembled. "It's right by the Yarra River. I think you'd like it."

"Melbourne? That's a long way away."

"Depends on your standpoint." He smiled. "Yves wouldn't mind. Would you, mate?" he called across the kitchen.

Yves looked at us, obviously caught unprepared. I hoped he would say "Yes, I would, very much so." I longed to hear him utter the words that would make me indispensable, even if as a joke.

"You've stooped low, stealing my chefs, Philippe. I won't allow it," Yves said instead.

I found his reaction, the tight grip of his fingers on the knife, ridiculous. Philippe was just teasing. He didn't mean for me to move to the other side of the world. I had no intention of changing countries yet again.

"Come now, Yves. You get a new crop from the school every year. The very best of the best. What's one chef? And she can decide for herself, *non*?"

Philippe's piercing blue eyes gleamed as he turned to me. He may have been friends with Yves, but there was more than a healthy amount of competition there as well. He was provoking him, and he meant it. He *was* inviting me to Melbourne. All of a sudden, I didn't know what to think. I was flattered, but Melbourne?

"Do you want to go?" Yves asked, his tone brusque. Both men were staring at me, one amused, one obviously striving to keep his composure and dominance.

All activity in the kitchen seemed to still in anticipation of my answer. It scared the life out of me at how powerful it made me feel—this chance to decide about my future, to decide about our future—and how much I liked it.

"I'd have to think about it." Even as I said it, I wasn't certain whether I just wanted to challenge Yves or if I meant it.

Yves's lips thinned into a sinister line. "*Bien*, she may go wherever she wants."

He threw his hands up and his anger concentrated in the white knuckles still gripping the knife.

"Yves." I went to hurry after him as he walked away, but Philippe stopped me with his hand on my shoulder.

"Forget him for a moment. Your career as a chef can blossom if you make the right choices," he said in a sweet, convincing voice. But I still longed for Yves's dry, caustic tone.

After the stand-off in the kitchen, Yves turned up at my place the next morning. His amiable sentiments towards Philippe seemed to have changed. He looked burdened with the events of the past week. The usually delicate white skin under his eyes was tender purple. Philippe's visit in the kitchen was not so much help as rivalry. Still, I could not imagine Yves having less taxing friendships. He couldn't stand half-heartedness.

I brewed coffee on my tabletop cooker and paid too much attention to the arrangement of the macarons as I placed them on a plate. He was standing by the window, his shoulder leaning on the frame. Pouring the coffee into mugs, I tensed up when I caught him gazing at me out of the corner of my eye.

Although he was obviously tired, his hand was steady when he accepted the mug and brought it to his lips. He closed his eyes as he took a sip and it made him look vulnerable. The moment passed quickly.

I caught him glancing at the sofa bed, but he didn't say anything.

Sex would have been a convenient distraction. But it was time we behaved like grown-ups. We had to get it out of the way first, whatever it was that had come between us. I supposed this was what happened when you left too much open space in a relationship. Tension and hurt colonised it.

"Are you thinking about going?" He sounded as though the words escaped him against his will and he would pull them back if he could.

"No."

"You were just trying to wind me up, then?"

"I was surprised by his offer, that's all." I was glad I

hadn't sat down at the table; it would have made me feel inferior, with him towering over me.

"Were you?" he asked, as if trying to provoke me.

"What's that supposed to mean?"

"You're talented." He paused. "You're a good worker; despite your inexperience, when it comes to teamwork, you have excellent leadership skills. You must have known sooner or later someone would try to lure you away with a good offer."

I opened my mouth but I didn't know what to say. I hadn't known that because I had never given it thought. I hadn't started cooking for a career, but it seemed that was what it had developed into and this baffled me. "I don't think I can handle the responsibility," I said, at last.

He looked me up and down, pensive. "You either can or you're out."

"What do you think I should do?"

He laughed humourlessly. "You're seriously asking me that?"

I had asked for advice he was more than fit to give so I didn't understand his surprise. "Why not?"

He stared at the floor, shaking his head and mumbling unintelligible French words for so long it started to irritate me.

"You want to know what I'd do?" he said, at last. "I'd get the word out that I was looking for a job and then I'd accept the best offer. I'd cook for the king of hell if it meant a promotion. But that's me."

"But it's not okay if I do the same?"

He hesitated for the briefest moment. "No. I don't want you to."

I had wanted to hear him say those same words the

previous evening. Little had changed in the few hours since then, but now the words somehow turned me into something less than him. As if I could not be my own person, but just an inferior part of a union. "Do you mean to say I'm not allowed to have a career because I'm with you? Because only one of us can put their job before everything else?" I walked to him, searching his face for proof I hadn't misunderstood. His reasoning was ludicrously unjust.

"I never promised to be fair."

"You never promised anything, Yves." I couldn't believe he'd think I'd be willing to give up everything when he wasn't willing to give up anything in return. That he would assume there was no limit to how much I was willing to put up with from him. Did he have so little respect that he valued me less than his job and expected me to like it? Silent and obedient until he was willing to let me go? So fucking little.

"What do you want from me? What were you expecting? A ring, three children, and an SUV? That's not me. I never deceived you," Yves said.

It was sad that after two years he knew so little about me that he could misjudge me so badly. But I supposed we were both responsible for that. Neither of us had been very forthcoming about personal things, either because we didn't want to make ourselves vulnerable, or because we were both too focused on our work to pay much attention to anything else. Possibly both.

"I just want to be treated as an equal. I've never wanted anything more."

"I told you, I cannot accept the same behaviour from you as I'd expect from myself. We're not the same."

"So you seem to think."

His eyes widened. He stood so close he was almost touching me.

"Where does that leave me, Yves? Where do I factor in in this relationship?" It was a blow that he cared so little about what I wanted. "Have I ever mattered to you at all?"

He opened his mouth and then closed it with a snap. We stared at each other for a long, tense moment.

"What do you want from me?" he asked again, voice tight, as if it were I who was at fault. He pressed his lips together. He looked ashen. I didn't know if it was from anger or shock or some other emotion entirely. This was so symptomatic of how he had always been with me that it didn't surprise me that even at such a critical moment I couldn't tell what he was thinking.

"*Entendu*," he said when I didn't respond. It was a whisper, yet it cut me to the core. "Philippe's number."

I couldn't fathom where he found the pencil, but he was already scribbling a number on the napkin on the kitchen table.

"Yves…"

His silence was frightening, but childish. I couldn't believe he would regress into such petulance.

He pushed past me towards the door. I tried grabbing his hand, but he wrenched it from my grasp.

I regretted I'd said I would think about Philippe's offer the day before. It had started as a joke and I hadn't thought it would come to this. But we had fought before and we had always made up.

I went through the rest of the day in a haze of disbelief. I turned up at the restaurant for my dinner shift. Philippe was no longer there, and I was told Yves was in his office.

Thoma handed me a note. "The Australian left this for you."

I hoped I imagined his reproach. But when afterwards he just walked away, I could no longer pretend.

I opened the note and stared at the Melbourne address a full minute. The events of the last twenty-four hours were beginning to feel real. It wasn't a good feeling because it was as though I no longer recognised my life, as though I'd borrowed it from someone else's bookshelf.

I knocked on the office door. Yves's "*Entrez*" sounded even sharper than the rap.

I knew he knew it was me, because when I stood in the doorway, he didn't look up. The deep lines on his forehead as he stared at the papers on the desk in front of him made him look unfamiliar. Yves wasn't usually troubled; he was either indifferent, focused, or angry.

"Yves," I said, but he raised his hand to silence me and kept reading and then picked up a pen and signed the paper.

At last, he looked at me and it seemed to pain him to do so. He pushed himself to his feet, sighing. Before I could start reasoning with him, he rounded the desk and handed me the papers he'd just signed. "Your last pay cheque and a letter of recommendation in case you don't end up going to Philippe," he said, his voice raspy.

I opened my mouth but nothing came out. I was being dismissed. After almost two years of being together, of working side by side, of giving him almost every minute of every day, I was being dismissed. As though none of it mattered. Yves no longer wanted me. God knows he had never needed me. I imagined, when I was gone, it would all be just as if I had never even been there. Not a trace of me left when I felt as though I'd left half of my soul behind in this kitchen.

Everything in me hurt. Tremors shook my body as I struggled to control myself. I felt cheated out of two years of my life. Just as I had started to think Yves maybe felt something for me, he was throwing me out on the street like the old dishwasher that had broken down last week. Found wanting and replaced.

"Yves…" My voice was awash with emotion and I hated he would see how weak I was. But I needn't have worried because he pushed past me and walked out into the kitchen. It was just another day at the restaurant: preparations needed to be finished; food needed to be cooked; I needed to get to my station.

Several plates were returned during the evening, but Yves didn't comment on my poor performance, possibly because it would have forced him to talk to me. In the bustling, noisy kitchen, I was alone. Yves demonstrated what it meant to be a leader—just by his example he had every person on the team ignore me as though I was a leper.

I started on the mise en place after closing time, although I was exhausted beyond belief. Irene walked up to me, tapping my shoulder. "You're free to go, Nina," she told me. "You won't be on the morning shift." Her dark eyes looked regretful but apart from wishing me good luck, she didn't say anything else.

Even as I was changing out of my uniform, I couldn't believe this was happening. I cleared out my locker, having to carry everything in my arms as I hadn't brought a bag. How was it possible I had been a valuable part of the team only yesterday and today I was being chased away like a traitor?

The night air was chilly when I opened the door, even though it was late May. I turned to look at the warm kitchen one last time. Yves stood at the front workstation at the other side of the long room, arms folded. His face was like a brewing storm, but I still couldn't deny how attracted I was to him. It struck me how beautiful he was, the black ink on his left arm trailing up under his white sleeve, his dark hair mussed from the rush of a long shift, his eyes tired and bottomless and seeming so angry with me. And then he turned and walked away.

I tried not to cry when I bumped into Thoma having a cigarette break, leaning against the wall outside. His heavy arms went around me. His comfort made me feel as though I was betraying them all.

"No regrets, Nina," he said. "Life goes on."

"I know," I croaked, but didn't really believe it.

"He's just upset that you're leaving," Thoma said, pulling away and shaking another cigarette from his pack. "You know what he's like. He's lashing out."

His words shook me. "But I don't want to leave," I blurted.

This made him pause but he didn't comment on it. He inhaled the first drag as if it were his lifeline. At last, he said, "It won't be the same here without you."

I knew nowhere else would be the same either. But it was too late to change things. If Yves didn't want me, I would not foist myself on him. I was too proud for that. "Thank you," I said.

All the way to my flat, I used my kitchen uniform to wipe away my tears. I unlocked the front door and wondered whether I would have done things differently if

I had known it would end like this. And I knew I wouldn't have.

There was a time in my life when I'd been repeatedly deserted by others: my emotionally unavailable parents, Marija, my grandfather, my first crush. I had vowed to myself then to get ahead of anyone planning to leave and do the leaving instead. I'd become good at it. I had left my mother and father in the end. I had left past boyfriends. Perhaps now it was time to leave Paris and Yves.

SEVEN

Melbourne was cold after Paris. But the heater in the taxi was going full blast until my legs felt burnt. The switch from end of May spring in Europe to late autumn in Australia was mindboggling.

I had a horrid taste in my mouth from the aeroplane food, and my eyes stung from lack of sleep. I had barely had rest since I had been let go four days before. During the flight, I couldn't stop thinking about my fight with Yves and I'd cried in the aeroplane toilet, until a mother thumped on the door, her five-year-old daughter needing to use the bathroom. I'd been mortified when the mother's eyes grew large at my tear-stained face when I emerged.

My body resented being thrown into the Australian winter without warning. I shivered as I walked from the taxi down a narrow lane and into the dark entrance to the building. When the door clunked shut behind me, it kept out the mix of the traffic noises and gentle ocean sounds across the road. The sudden silence of the lobby jarred.

Everything about this place felt strange. With the hasty departure, I'd had no time to prepare for the move. I didn't know what to expect. Most of the things I knew about Melbourne came from Philippe. I was used to the elegant buildings of Paris and the narrow old streets, and what I'd seen of Melbourne on the way from the airport looked flat and unfamiliar.

I dragged my suitcase up the stairs. On the way, I'd stopped at the estate agent's to pick up the key. The fee for the flat I'd rented was considerable seeing how small it had seemed in the photos. I pushed the door open. My breath caught in my throat and I almost cried again, but this time with relief. The place wasn't a hole as I'd feared. The photos hadn't even hinted at how light and airy it was with its high ceilings. I dropped the suitcase by the door. The balcony door creaked as I opened it; its paint was peeling and tiny flakes peppered the hardwood floor, turning pink in the setting sun. I stepped out onto the small balcony off the bedroom, tiled and empty, and took a deep breath. It felt like my first breath for a very long time.

The kitchen was the largest room, with a quality stainless steel sink but a cooker rusty around the edges and missing a button. I would have to stock the empty cupboards. The whining the fridge made when I plugged it in reminded me of myself in the morning, complaining about having to get up.

My suitcase contained barely enough clothes to fill two drawers out of the four large ones in the chest in the bedroom. Two years before, when I had moved to Paris, I was still grieving my mother's death. Even so, excitement had bubbled in me as I'd unpacked my suitcases in that studio apartment. I'd been full of anticipation of a new life, the hope of all the good things to come. Here, I had the promise of a good job and a new start, yet I couldn't muster up much enthusiasm. The thought of what I'd left behind in Paris made me feel too wretched. But after twenty-four hours wallowing in misery on the aeroplane,

I refused to think of Yves.

Unused to the soft mattress, I was awake most of the night. I couldn't find a comfortable position, until everything hurt and I got up around three to make instant coffee I'd bought at the airport and watch the sun rise over the city. The traffic light from the street alternated between reflecting green and red and yellow in my window. The sea beyond the narrow stretch of sand on the other side of the road swelled dark and lazy and palm trees rustled in the breeze. I opened the window and inhaled the chilly night air with its smell of salt and the flowers of the camellia shrub in the garden below. Faced with a scene like that, things didn't feel so bleak. Perhaps living so far from Yves would help me get over him and his dismissal.

In the morning, I entered the address Philippe had left with Thoma in the GPS map on my phone. My start and end points were connected by a fairly straightforward green line. I was restless and needed to move, so I decided to walk to Southbank rather than take a taxi. I set off in the direction of the Yarra River, as the GPS suggested.

I reached a large crossroads and was no longer sure which way to go. I turned on the spot, taking in the surroundings. I hadn't noticed until then how vast it all was. The street was lined with low bungalows. Compared to Paris, the houses were large and it seemed extravagant for a single family home to take so much space in a city where space was a precious commodity.

A belt of grass and trees between the pavement and the road created that awkward mix where the greenery tried to convince you that you were close to nature, in an almost rural environment, but how regulated it all was clearly suggested a city. I had always thought of suburbia as fake, pretending to be something other than it was. It was neither as wild as the village I had grown up in, nor as cultured as the city proper. The saving grace of this inner suburb was the beach and the proximity of my new workplace.

What would my father think of this place? I hadn't called him to tell him I was moving to Melbourne. I should have, but what if it didn't work out? There was no point upsetting him yet. I would have to call him eventually, though. My empty stomach constricted at the thought.

The houses gave to tall office buildings, galleries, and museums; there was more traffic, but surprisingly, the greenery persisted and reminded me of Luxembourg Gardens where I had once encountered Yves. But the smells were all wrong—minty and salty, with a hint of honey.

I came out of my daydream when a car almost ran me over as I crossed the street because I checked for traffic to my left instead of my right. Another reminder I was no longer in Europe. Once I got used to the left-hand traffic, I would have to consider buying a car. Distances in Australia were not what I was used to: I had misjudged how far I had to walk, and it took me an hour to reach Philippe's bistro.

As I stood at the entrance, a crippling nervousness made my hands tremble and my legs weak. Had I done a stupid thing coming here after I'd built a life for myself in Paris? Did I even have the energy to start all over again? If I talked to Yves, apologised to him, perhaps we could sort things out. But for what? To remain in a relationship where I and my job would always come second to him? A joint future didn't seem likely, or even smart, but even so I missed Yves with an intensity that made me ache.

I pushed the door and found it unlocked. I walked in. The kitchen was on my left and it was barely lit as the workday had not yet started. It looked half the size of the one I'd just come from. Maybe that was why I thought it welcoming. That and the polished worksurfaces, which spoke of a good work ethic and high standards—something I was used to from Paris.

A clanking noise from behind a partition wall was the only sign the place was occupied. A spotlight lit a part of the worksurface. It had a cutting board on it and a piece of cheese with a large knife stuck in it as if someone had wanted to cut a slice and then changed their mind.

"May I help you?"

I jumped when the voice came from my right, out of the dimness of the dining area. I had thought all the activity was focused behind the partition wall, but there was someone laying the tables in the far corner. It took me a second look to realise it was a man. The ropey dreadlocks were deceiving.

"I'm looking for Philippe," I said.

"He isn't in yet. Can I help?"

When he came closer, he turned out to be quite young. Four or five years younger than me, I thought.

"I'm... He..." I had expected to deal with Philippe directly. "We discussed a job."

"My arse on toast!" said a smoky voice to my left. I turned to see a short, red-haired woman next to the cutting board.

"E-excuse me?" I said.

"What happened to you?" she asked when she came closer. "You look as if you've gone a few rounds with Buffy."

The young man chuckled.

I must have looked as confused as I felt. I hadn't slept in days and my muscles were still in spasm from being zipped up in an economy seat for twenty-four hours. I was in no shape to deal with Dreadlocks and Buffy and I needed time to pull myself together.

"Rennie, stop scaring her," the man said. "I'm Jeff, and this is Miren, the sous-chef. You'll be the new chef, I reckon."

Before I could respond, Miren went on, "Did you come here straight from the airport? You need sleep and food."

"I arrived yesterday," I said, defensive.

"You still need sleep and food. Come," she said, motioning for me to follow.

When Jeff chuckled again, I felt small and weak. I had come here to be the chef of the restaurant and I was being bossed around on my first day. What a joke.

"You can't go wrong trusting her. Go on," Jeff said.

Miren served me onion soup and a cheeseboard and she never stopped talking while I ate. I sat on a rickety chair by the worksurface while she prepared bacon and cheese for breakfast. I told her where I was from, and she told me about her parents who had moved from the Basque country to Australia in the eighties when she was just three years old. After her father lost work on the sugar cane plantations up north, they'd moved to Melbourne.

"I hated the move, the temperamental weather, the city life," Miren said, while I soaked up the soup with a piece of bread. "Then I accepted it. I stayed even when I could have left."

Every other sentence was about her two teenaged sons. I began to suspect her family was the reason she had no ambition of being promoted to a chef. "I prefer to run things in the background."

Her story was interrupted by Philippe's arrival. Philippe's moustache grew exuberantly under his thin nose. His face would have been the perfect logo for his French bistro, but for me, his presence was a shadow from Paris. I tried to suppress the memories of him laughing and joking with Yves as they cooked and of Yves's livid face when he left my flat. Had that really happened just days ago? I swallowed hard.

"Aaah, you came," he said. When he smiled, there was his victory over Yves in his eyes, but genuine pleasure, too.

He showed me the kitchen, which was waking up with noise and smells, and introduced the staff who trickled in one by one. The pace was calmer than in Paris, the boss less severe.

"Can you start tomorrow?"

I nodded. Finally, I felt excitement. But there was a sad undertone. I couldn't help but think of Yves and how I might have still been working alongside him.

It took me a few months to get used to the slower rhythm of life, and the weather, which was more capricious than anywhere else I'd lived. One morning, I woke up to clear blue skies, and by early afternoon, the temperatures were in the mid-twenties, but then the sky dimmed and an evening downpour chilled the atmosphere so I had to put my duvet, or doona as Miren called it, back on the bed. While Miren complained about the weather, I liked how unpredictable it was.

On a day in October, I crossed the wide Yarra River, trapped between the concrete riverbanks. Its colour reminded me of the river back home, which was so often like a café latte after prolonged rains. But there, the river would spill onto its banks and rise towards our garden until we watched anxiously to see if it was going to flood the house. In contrast, the Yarra seemed tamed by the concrete banks, somehow docile and slow. I wondered if it ever showed its true force, and if I would stay long enough to witness it. A part of me dreamed of returning to Paris and Yves, but another part hoped this city might become home. That I could settle here, at last. Yet every time I thought that, I was reminded of my village and father, living alone in that old house. I hadn't been back in three years. What would the place be like now?

Often after work, I walked around to lose myself and relax my feverish brain. Although rush hours in the kitchen gave me deep satisfaction, the leftover adrenaline coursing my body wouldn't let me rest. Even when I finished my shift in the middle of the night, it took me hours to go to sleep.

Professional cooking was like an extreme sport, with the exhilaration and exhaustion which followed a hard day at work. I craved that adrenaline rush, the excitement, and how it took courage to persist day to day. It was like a never-ending competition with oneself, trying to outdo the success of the day before with an even bigger coup. That was one thing Yves and I had in common. Regardless of how tired he was, every well-served dish filled him with gratification. How right he had been when he recognised that same passion in me long before I even suspected I had it in me to become a chef. How good it had felt to have someone who knew me so well.

But I imagined that after years of living and breathing cooking, it would drain you. Perhaps that was why Yves preferred to work in a mid-range restaurant these days because he was aware he was too old to keep up with the sparkling new chefs emerging onto the culinary scene. I wondered if it bothered him, getting old and losing his edge.

Unlike Yves, Philippe was more laid-back. He had never achieved the same success as Yves, but he seemed happier. Every day, he returned to his family and forgot about the kitchen, while Yves never stopped to pause and rest. Two chefs, two styles. I vacillated somewhere in between, not quite sure what I wanted.

It was starting to upset me how memories of Yves sneaked up on me at the most unexpected moments. I dwelled on them until they hurt so much I had to pause and take a deep breath. It happened more often after long, difficult shifts.

I'd finished the morning shift four hours before and I was still buzzing, unwilling to return to my small flat where I couldn't move about. I wandered down a street where a line of patrons was being served out of a caravan café. Mason jars with fairy lights were suspended above the tables. They would have looked quite magical at night. Potted plants lined the shelves along the wall, artificial flowers covered the caravan, and AstroTurf was laid underfoot. It was all a bit kitschy, which I wouldn't usually like, but the unpretentious menu, DIY-type design, and the fact that it was tucked into an alley made it all work.

There was quite a crowd in front of the caravan, from

the business district suits to youngsters with earbuds pushed in and nodding to music.

I ordered a pie and coffee and carried them to a small red table. Only when I sat did I realise how heavy and tired my feet were from hours of standing at work and the long walk.

I sighed with relief and looked about. Could you call it getting lost when you ended up in such a perfect spot? Yves had once asked me why I was so afraid of making a mistake when I hesitated over searing a Dover sole. "Mistakes feel delicious right up to the point they turn out to be mistakes," he had said. "And then they offer you the chance to learn a lesson. All in all, mistakes are good for you. Embrace them. Make them."

I had laughed in his face. Now, I glanced around, marvelling at the events that had brought me here. Perhaps there were no mistakes, just a rather lengthy process of discovery.

I pulled my jacket tighter around me when a gust of air ruffled my hair and the suspended lamps swayed above my head. Spring in Melbourne could be chilly.

"How're you going?" someone said.

I turned at the sound. An older man sat at the next table, wrinkles creasing his sunburnt skin. "Excuse me?" I said.

"Just asking how's things, miss, if you don't mind." He smiled and added a few lines to his cheeks. "You looked sad just then," he continued, when I didn't reply.

Did I? I had been thinking about Yves, true. "I'm well, thanks. Just tired. How was your day?"

"Slow," he said, his fingers playing with a sugar packet. "I'm not used to the city," he added, although I hadn't asked for an explanation. "I'm Walt." He stretched out his chunky hand and I grasped it in mine.

"Nina." His grip was firm, verging on painful, skin like sandpaper. "New to Melbourne?" His accent was Australian, I was sure of it, but he might have moved here from a different place.

"Aye. Used to live in Gawler. But me daughter Neroli lives here."

"You came here to be closer to her?" I asked, thinking of how far away from my father I had moved. I couldn't remember whether his face was as wrinkled as this man's. I'd called him twice in the five months since I'd moved to Melbourne. I still wondered what had been going through his mind during the pause that followed my telling him I was in Australia. His soft words, when he finally said, "I hope you'll be happy there," filled me with crippling guilt.

"She wants me here," the old man now said, disrupting my thoughts. He rubbed his cheek with his hand. "I had a farm, small one, mind you, but she says now Imogen's gone, I better stay close to her in case…" He cleared his throat. "Well, you know. When someone our age dies, children think we'll start dropping like flies. But you're too young to understand. Too young." He fidgeted with the sugar packet until it tore and the sugar bled out. "Blimey," he said, his hands trembling as he tried to scoop the sugar into his palm.

He looked out of place in this hipster environment. But I could easily envisage him eating apricot chicken straight from the casserole at a solid oak table with a view of the paddocks out the kitchen window.

I had rarely allowed myself to think about my father because I then reproached myself for leaving him alone in the old house, with only his neighbour, Mrs Vidic, for company. I told myself he was fine, he wasn't so old, after all, and he'd always been more than capable of taking care of himself. He didn't need my help, never had, not the way I had needed him as a little girl when the inexplicable conflicts between my parents confused and frightened me.

"I'm not close to my father," I said out of the blue, surprising as much myself as the old man.

He didn't seem to know what to say to my words, and I was sorry I had spoken. "He lives far away," I added. I made it sound as though he was the one who'd left, so I corrected myself, "I moved here from Europe. For work."

"My! Maybe it's me poor hearing, but I took you for an Aussie."

Ever since I'd left home, I had communicated in English. The pocket dictionary in my bag was like a reminder that I had the language on loan. The dictionary was dog-eared from when I had thumbed it daily in Sweden. In Paris, French had become handier because of the cookery terms and because the French wouldn't speak English. And here, the dictionary was of little use to me when everyone used words so peculiar, I sometimes suspected they made them up. Jeff, for example, had said a small heater under the bar was cactus, and for weeks I thought that was his pet name for the heater. Then I heard Philippe tell him he'd finally called a repairman for the *broken* heater. Or Miren had asked me just yesterday if it wasn't too cold for thongs, and I wondered where she'd got the idea I wore thongs, until I realised she was staring at my flip-flops and wasn't referring to my underwear.

Navigating in a new language was a lot like exploring

a city without a map. I got lost, I embarrassed myself, I received confused glances, and more than once I'd been frustrated when unable to express exactly what I wanted to say. But embracing the language was key if I wanted to fit in. I had quickly given up trying to speak correctly. Instead, I imitated Miren and Jeff and used their delightfully odd expressions, sometimes aptly, sometimes making mistakes that had Miren roaring with laughter. But after five months, it was getting easier and I was more and more comfortable. With Miren from the Basque country, Philippe from Paris, and Jeff with his Aboriginal roots, I fit in just by being me.

From time to time, when I used an expression I hadn't known a few months before, I wondered at myself. Who was this person, pronouncing words like "tucker" and "arvo" as though I'd been saying them my whole life; making friends as I learned to surf on the beaches south of Melbourne; sometimes staying up late at the bar with Miren and Jeff, occasionally even Philippe, chatting and laughing like I hadn't chatted and laughed in years? Perhaps ever.

The easy acceptance of my workmates and the adventure of a new place, and a new culture, swept me up in a whirlwind of enjoyment. So much that when I had called my father last time, I greeted him in English, and he'd almost disconnected the call before I realised my mistake.

"I've picked up some expressions from my workmates," I said now.

"Where do you work?" Walt asked. Now the focus had shifted from him to me, his fingers stilled in his lap.

"I cook in a bistro, in Southbank."

"A cook? Good on ya."

I smiled. I liked his expressive face. That he found his situation difficult made me feel for him. I had struggled to find my place most of my life. I knew what he was going through, and at his age. I wanted to tell him it would be all right, but even I wasn't sure I believed that.

"We call it a chef so it sounds grander."

He chuckled. "I bet a bloke came up with that nonsense 'cause he hated being called a cook."

"I bet."

"What's the place called? I might come try your cooking sometime," he said, eagerly.

"Please do. I'll make you something special." I made a promise I wasn't sure I could keep but I couldn't stop talking. I wanted to make him feel better, less lost. I wanted to show him I was a "blow-in", too. "I'll make you something from my old country," I said, and memories clouded my thoughts. What was I thinking? I never cooked anything with a whiff of my mother's kitchen. For years, I had actively worked to forget her recipes. The thought of using them now tempted me to take back my words.

When he promised he would visit, seeming pleased, almost grateful for the invitation I'd extended, I wished I had kept my mouth shut.

I had never lived this close to the ocean, and for the first few weeks, its sounds kept me awake at night. Once I got used to it, the swooshing waves turned into a relaxing therapy after intense shifts at the bistro. I took a dip in the bay almost daily when the weather became warmer in the spring.

The closer we got to the height of summer, the more crowded the beach was, the noise of the people and the waves creating a sort of aural fireworks. I liked to sit in the sand and watch the ocean fall with a satisfied sigh, like me after a tiring day. Just as it was about to rest on the sand, it was pulled back by restless energy. Back to the grind, the constant ebb and flow, the endless churning motion, as if it craved the freedom of the high seas but couldn't quite tear away from dry land.

Having the warm, welcoming ocean at my feet was a comfort. I had always loved water. I spent my childhood summers on the riverbank, diving in the chilly water to wash off the sweat and heat, collecting pebbles and making sculptures out of them in the shade of the garden, drawing maps of my world in the fine river sand—all of them washed away by high water in the end.

But the river couldn't be compared to the endless ocean. The first few times I'd stepped into the sea with apprehension. But as I watched the surfers every morning and the ease with which they tamed the ocean I became more daring. Once I tried surfing, however, it turned out, as things often did, it wasn't quite how I had imagined. It certainly wasn't as easy as it looked at first glance.

I'd missed the prime surfing season between March and September, but since I was a newbie, or "shark biscuit" as my instructor called me with a grin, I could find suitable waves at any time of the year. I booked surfing lessons on the western beaches of Phillip Island. My excitement waned a bit when I had to suffer a two-hour bus ride to get there. I bought a second-hand Hyundai in October, and it became easier to dash off to San Remo in the morning, cross the bridge to the island, and return at the end of the day.

Once I got the hang of it and I dared to try bigger waves, I took the highway to Sorrento on Mornington Peninsula almost every day I was off work. I still wiped out—surf-speak for falling off my board, as I learned the first time—three times out of four, but my strong chef's arms meant I could paddle like the best of them. When I rode a wave to the shore, people stared as I rejoiced and skipped across the sand with pleasure. But it wasn't in one of those proud moments I made my first surfing friends. It was after a nasty wipe-out when a local, Jim, helped me get to the shore and introduced me to his gang. Although surfing was hard and I discovered with the onset of muscle soreness that I had muscles I hadn't known about, it was worth the effort if only for this camaraderie and the sublime feeling of taming the waves.

Even on days I couldn't afford to go to Sorrento, I made a detour to the beach and watched the swimmers, the gentle waves in the bay, and boats whizzing past, to and from Docklands. The harbour was simultaneously their sanctuary and a door out into the world.

There was something to be said for exploring the world, I thought. It painted home from a different perspective. It made it clear to me home should provide me with what the harbour did for boats—refuge and freedom at the same time. I'd been unable to find either in my homeland, so I'd moved.

Two years before, ten months into my cookery course, I had told Yves how strange it was when I returned home for my mother's funeral after being away for five years.

"All this running away is childish, even you have to admit that," he had said.

"I'm not running away. Travelling gave me a new perspective on my starting point. I just didn't know it until I went back."

"Starting point? You can't even say the word home."

His mocking hurt, but I would never admit it. "I haven't yet decided where that is," I told him, and I believed it. He didn't seem convinced, so I said, "You've moved, too. Where is your home, then?"

He'd told me his mother was of Polish descent. I didn't know whether he had ever visited her homeland or if he wanted to, but of course he'd lived in America as well as a child.

"My home is where I am," he said, touching his hand to his chest.

If he was right, perhaps it was because of all the confusion inside me that I couldn't find a home. But surely it couldn't be as simple as me deciding on where I wanted my home to be?

For now, I liked Melbourne. It accepted you, but it let you go, too, if you wanted to.

The aromas reminded me of my mother as Miren wiped the remnants of spices from the worksurface in front of her. Dinner preparations were in full swing. Usually, the rhythm of a busy kitchen sucked me in and cleared my mind of everything else. But today my thoughts kept drifting. I thought of how my mother had never used allspice in her kitchen. Perhaps she hadn't even known it existed. I thought of my promise to cook a Slovenian dish for Walt. Why had I made such a careless offer? How could I cook anything Slovenian when I hadn't done so in years? I'd probably forgotten the recipes. Even if I hadn't,

I wouldn't feel comfortable doing it. That was no longer part of me and it would just stir up unwanted memories. I had been stupid to make a promise to Walt. But there was something about him, I realised, that had touched me. Reminded me of my father, perhaps. Or maybe it was just that I felt bad for not calling home more often and I had tried to compensate for that by being nice to a complete stranger.

"Did I tell you about Mark?" Miren asked, all of a sudden.

I looked up and shook my head. "Who's Mark?"

"I met him at the apartment building where I used to live. He's an expat."

Somehow I knew what she was going to say next. I stifled my sigh.

"He's Slovenian, like you," she told me over a heap of julienned carrots. "Well, his father was, I think."

"Where from?"

Miren made a face and shrugged.

I didn't care for meeting other Slovenians, not now when I kept thinking of home and my father living alone.

"Tell me about him," I said, knowing she would anyway. I couldn't escape to a different part of the kitchen while preparing the meat, my fingers sticky with the mixture of olive oil, salt, pepper, and honey.

"He works for a consulting firm, environmental or something. He bores me when he talks about it, so I don't listen." Miren had a habit of rounding out her vowels. In her mouth, words became fat and juicy. Her voice was deep and husky and she sounded as if she were discussing something grave and significant even when she talked about her choice of sandwich. "We went to the cinema a few times. Had a good laugh, drinks afterwards. He can hold his drink, I can tell you. He'd be perfect for you." She grinned, still chopping vegetables.

"I don't pick men according to how much they can drink," I said, irked. I'd mentioned once how prevalent alcoholism was in Slovenia, and apparently she thought I condoned the habit.

"Just teasing, girl," Miren said with a patronising voice that suggested she was much older than me, but there were only seven years between us. "And I only meant for you to meet him. He's one of you, that's all. And he's a good bloke."

"I'm sorry. Bad day."

"Something happened?"

"It was my father's birthday yesterday, and I didn't call him."

Miren stopped chopping and looked up.

"What do I say to him, Ren?" I asked, even though I didn't expect her to have a solution. "I don't know how to speak to him anymore. We've been drifting apart for years. Last time I called, we were on the phone for three minutes. Half of that, we were silent."

"So you're just going to ignore him?"

I set the bowl of marinade onto the worksurface with more force than necessary. "I'm afraid that whatever I do, he'll get the wrong impression. If I don't call, he'll think I've forgotten about him. If I call, it'll sound forced because I've nothing genuine to say." I washed my hands under hot water until they turned red. "I don't handle these things well, relationships. I'm good at cooking, I excel at braising steaks, and I can fillet fish any time, day or night. I like folding fitted sheets. Swimming and surfing, I love those. These things calm me. I enjoy them. I want to just do that and not think about other stuff. I want life to stop bothering me. Shit."

Miren hurried to put the julienne into the tray by her side when Philippe entered the kitchen. He nodded at us on his way to the maitre d'.

"It upsets my stomach," I grunted. "It won't even let me enjoy the things I like. Everything becomes mechanical and full of guilt." The knives and forks clanged with resentment as I dropped them into the sink.

"Call Mark, go for a drink. He speaks Slovenian, I think. Maybe it'll help you to reconnect."

I agreed to meet Mark because I didn't want to offend Miren. But that didn't stop me from thinking about my father and, oddly, about Walt. He probably celebrated his birthday with his daughter and her family, if she had one, unlike my father who didn't have any family left, apart from me. Maybe my father had celebrated with his friends. Did he have friends left? Not knowing the answer made me feel like an awful, heartless daughter.

After my shift, I spent an hour in the storeroom where I sorted through the produce and other ingredients, but rather than organising them, I kept thinking about the dishes my mother cooked when I was young.

Between Walt, my father's birthday, and Miren suggesting I meet another expat, cooking for Walt was the easiest thing to cope with. I thought about which recipes I could remember from home. At first, I couldn't think of a single one. Then, I remembered my mother's advice from when I had wanted to learn to cook when I was six or seven. "Start with something simple," she used to say.

A dish made with three ingredients was simple

enough. I cracked an egg into a small quantity of flour in a bowl. After adding a pinch of salt, I mixed it all with a fork and then continued with my fingers until the flour and egg formed small clumps. I boiled them in milk, letting it bubble and simmer on the hob until it thickened into the creamy pudding I'd adored as a child. I scooped a spoonful out of the pot and blew on it before I tasted it. It was the sort of comfort food I imagined an old, lonely man might like.

Yves would probably think it too basic, but I wished I could cook it for him anyway. I just wished I could stare in his dark eyes and hear his voice, even if he told me my cooking was below par. But he was thousands of kilometres away and probably hadn't thought of me once since I'd left.

Mark turned out to be friendly, like most Australians I had met over the past eight months. He asked where I'd like to meet, and I suggested the Eureka Skydeck, one of the highest skyscrapers in the southern hemisphere, which I hadn't yet managed to visit.

I told him, in the Eureka elevator, that my parents' entire village could be crammed into this one building, and he laughed too loudly. I felt exposed when everyone turned to stare at us. I'd already had my misgivings about this meeting. Now the feeling only intensified.

"My *tata*"—he put the stress on the second syllable, and I only understood the word once I heard the rest of the sentence—"came here after the war. I think he might have been running from the communist secret police. He never told me, but I once heard him talk about it with my aunt," Mark said.

The elevator stopped and we followed the crowd, mostly tourists, down a short, dim hallway. Mark didn't stop talking. "A few years after he arrived, he got a local girl pregnant and had to marry her. My older brother was born four months later. I wasn't planned either. Ma and Dad divorced soon after my birth."

A family history told by enumerating its sins. I smiled politely, confused by his willingness to share his family's unhappy story. With the few pleasant memories I had of my family, I preferred not to talk about it at all. I had only told Yves about my past well into our relationship.

The vista from the bar at the top of the Eureka Tower was indeed amazing. Melbourne was a big city, but the view was unencumbered by smog. The ocean breezes helped, and yesterday's rain had cleansed the sultry atmosphere. I loved how often it rained here.

"Do you speak any Slovenian?" I asked as we sat at a table in the bar and gave our order.

"*Malo*," he said.

"Are you close to your father?"

He shook his head. "Alec, my brother, died in a boating accident when he was sixteen. I was twelve at the time. My father moved up to Deniliquin after the accident. I don't see him much."

"I'm sorry."

"Where's your family?"

"It's just me and my father. Not close either."

"Geographically or…"

"Both."

The waitress brought us our drinks. Coffee for Mark, a glass of water for me as I'd had too much coffee already. Jittery fingers didn't mix well with a chef's knife.

"What little Slovenian I speak, it's from my father's sister, Ana," Mark said. "She followed him here a few years after he left. She and Ma raised us, and I still go to my aunt's place every Sunday for lunch. She never had a family of her own, so she doted on Alec and me. Ana is the most generous person I know."

He didn't seem to expect a response from me. So I let him talk while I only half listened and sipped the cold water. Mark didn't appear to resent his father for leaving him when he was still a child; he accepted it with surprising grace. His congeniality and openness were in such contrast to Yves's surliness and aloofness. I couldn't help compare them. It had been months, yet I missed Yves just as much as when I had got off the plane in May.

I doused the ache with the remaining cold water. To his credit, Mark recognised that as a sign I was ready to leave.

"You should come visit Ana with me," he said.

I glanced at my wristwatch. My shift started in an hour.

"I meant some other time. A Sunday, for lunch. You might like how Slovenian she still is even after living here for decades."

"I wouldn't want to impose."

"You wouldn't be." This time, he didn't understand my reluctance, or pretended not to.

The air was warm and thick with moisture as I waited for Mark in front of Flinders Street Station on a Sunday in February. I'd never ridden the tram before, so we took it to Hawthorn Station and then walked the last part of the way to Ana's. The pungent aroma of coffee was in the air as we passed a coffee roaster. Businesses and bars followed, until we entered a narrow residential street.

Mark had said his father was from Bohinj, an Alpine oasis of pristine nature, fresh air, and icy clear water. I couldn't imagine what Ana must have thought of this beehive of house upon house in neatly delineated rows. I had heard of immigrants who tried desperately to rebuild their home environments decades after their arrival in a foreign land, creating a carbon copy of Slovenia abroad. I couldn't imagine being so restricted, defined exclusively by my origins and culture.

Mark and I had chatted all the way from the tram station, but now we both fell silent. Perhaps Mark was nervous about taking me with him to meet the woman who was like a mother to him. I wondered if I'd made a mistake coming here. We'd only gone out a couple of times and this visit seemed too meaningful. As if I were promising him something more. But it was too late, too rude, to turn back now.

Despite the traffic noise in the distance, barely a car passed on a Sunday in this area. The pavement glittered with the remains of the early morning shower. The sun dislodged a bank of clouds and shone through, bright against the grey backdrop. I breathed in the air infused with the tangy smell of eucalyptus. I had come to like the scent.

I took two more steps before I realised Mark had stopped.

"Here we are," he said. "Ready?" But he knocked without waiting for my reply.

The door was opened by a small, delicate old woman. She was dressed in a white blouse with a lacy collar and dark blue skirt. I felt underdressed in my jeans and t-shirt.

Even before Mark introduced us, I smelled beef broth. The smell was different to any in my kitchen but it reminded me of my mother's cooking and I suddenly had a hollow feeling in the pit of my stomach. Perhaps I wasn't as ready as I'd thought.

"Hello, Ana." Mark bent low and kissed Ana's cheek. "This is Nina. She's from your old country."

Immediately, Ana reverted to our mother tongue with gusto. "*Dobrodošla. Počuti se kot doma*," she said, her high-pitched voice revealing her surprise, perhaps pleasure.

"*Hvala.*" I wasn't sure how I had expected to feel speaking my native tongue face to face with a fellow Slovenian after all this time, but I didn't expect it to make me so emotional. It was as if I'd gone back in time and I was a child again. Slightly frightening, raw, but not entirely unpleasant.

In a way, I had been hiding behind a foreign language, but I was now exposed by my mother tongue, standing naked, unprotected, without the shield of the detachment English had offered me. I felt comfortable at its familiarity but also vulnerable and unnerved. I wished Mark would join in the conversation so we'd have to revert to English. I needed time to process this change. I needed to immerse myself in my mother tongue slowly, word by word rather than plunge in, gasping for breath.

I entered the living room, which could have been my family living room from twenty-five years before. The similarity to my childhood home was surreal—the crucifix in the corner, the bobbin lace curtains, the crocheted tablecloth on the low rectangular coffee table, and the glass-fronted cupboard with shelves filled with what were no doubt spirits.

My heart sped as I took it all in, expecting memories to flood me. A crumpled blanket in the corner of the sofa, a pair of glasses on the table, a piece of fabric with a partially embroidered rose next to them. The room looked lived-in, unlike the living room back home, which had been off limits to me as a child. Even though the two rooms were almost identical, the atmosphere was entirely different.

"Feels a bit like Slovenia," I said in English, for Mark's benefit.

I leaned closer to Mark and whispered, gesturing to the shelves, "We display alcoholic beverages like the Americans display their diplomas."

Mark's suppressed laugh sounded like a whimper, but Ana was oblivious. With characteristic insistent hospitality, she ordered us to sit on the sofa and wait for lunch. I kept feeling the urge to laugh, not entirely out of derision. It was surprisingly pleasant, this piece of Slovenia abroad.

"Is she eccentric or what?" Mark said, once Ana retreated to the kitchen.

"She's Slovenian."

His eyes crinkled when he laughed. I was getting used to his hearty, loud laugh. Yves had barely cracked a smile.

"Lunch is always the same," Mark said.

"Soup, sautéed potatoes, steak, green salad." I smiled when his eyes widened. "Does she at least offer wine?"

"And grappa after dessert," he said.

"Of course," I said, thinking of my grandfather, who had also always drunk a shot of grappa following Sunday lunch.

Melbourne stirred all sorts of feelings in me almost from the beginning. Here, unlike in Paris, I had a life outside of the restaurant kitchen. It was as if my eyes were truly open for the first time as I strolled the city, past famous landmarks, cafés, churches, and parks. Maybe that was part of the reason I felt more at home here. But I also often—too often for my liking—thought of my parents' village. Here, now, laughing at how familiar this was to me, made me homesick.

Mark and I moved the few steps from the sofa to the table once Ana brought out the tureen. The house was small and the dining table tucked against the living room wall, right next to the kitchen doorway. It was obvious Ana didn't get many visitors as there was only space for three people around the table. I wondered how many Australian friends she had made over the years.

Although lunch was why Mark and I had visited, the meal took second place to all the questions Ana had for me. Mark had finished his soup before I managed to taste mine.

"How are things back home?" Ana asked.

"I haven't been home in three years," I said.

"Why?" She stopped eating as she watched me. I had nothing to say because whatever answer I came up with, I could tell it would never justify me not visiting our home country regularly. "If I were as young as you, I'd go back every year. Perhaps I'd just go back for good," she said.

Her wistful tone touched me, even though our views differed. She remembered Slovenia as a dreamland because she was probably forced to leave it. I left of my own free will because it was not a dreamland for me.

"Things are not exactly great back home," I said, trying

to make her see she had no reason to pine for our home country. When she'd left, we were still part of Yugoslavia. "They've struggled since independence. As far as I know, the financial crisis hit them hard. Crime's gone up; the quality of life has plummeted for everyone but the very rich. My father can barely survive on his pension these days." When my mother died, I offered to send him money from Sweden every month. That would have been easier than worrying about him and feeling bad for not staying. He'd declined, saying he had some money stashed in a sock under his bed.

I glanced at Mark and he smiled, absentmindedly playing with the salt cellar.

Ana waved her hand. "I don't care about politics. I miss the people and the landscapes of Gorenjska."

I often marvelled at the vastness of the Australian landscape compared with my constrictive home valley. Even the colours here were different to those at home— the green was not the same shade, the river couldn't compare to the ocean blue, and there was a lot more yellow and ochre in Melbourne, while back home the mountains added fir green, brown, grey, in winter even white, to the palette.

While memories of the Slovenian landscape triggered conflicting feelings in me, it was always at the back of my mind: a benchmark to compare all other landscapes to. Perhaps that was why I chose to live in cities. There were more than twice as many people living in Melbourne than in the whole of Slovenia. One could hardly compare that.

"Mark tells me you're a cook. Don't be too harsh on my cooking, eh?" There was a tinge of nervousness in Ana's smile. Or maybe it was a warning.

"You've cooked the perfect Slovenian Sunday lunch," I said.

This propelled her to her feet and she carried our empty soup plates to the kitchen and then started piling my plate with potatoes, steak, and gravy.

"Thank you. There's no way I'll be able to eat all that," I said.

"Nonsense."

My cheeks flushed. It was poor form to leave food on the plate, and I was dismayed at the staggering heap on mine. I wasn't used to eating before noon, particularly not after a late shift. I was destined to either suffer with stomach ache and reflux or make a bad first impression.

I looked to Mark for help.

"A chef who doesn't eat," he said, grinning. "I'll help you with that."

"I eat, just not this early. When I work late, I get up later than this. Breakfasts are not my thing."

"That's just wrong," Ana said. "You young people have it all backwards—going to bed too late, getting up when half the day is already over. When you have a family, you'll have to mend your ways."

I focused on not glancing at Mark. Ana was not so subtle, and she looked pointedly at him, her eyebrows raised as if it was his responsibility to get me back on track. If lunch had started with the charm of nostalgia, it was quickly becoming awkward. Ana might have spent the best part of her life in Melbourne, but that hadn't rid her of the terrible habit of meddling I remembered from back home.

"The late hours are part of my job," I said to break the uneasy silence. "Besides, I think here people go out to dinner at a more reasonable time than back home. When I was a teenager, it was all the rage to go to a party as late in the evening as possible."

Ana was obviously disappointed either with me or the entire world when she said, "I may be old and have lost touch with the world, but I think that's just foolish."

Since I didn't know whether she meant my explanation or the general state of things, I kept quiet.

"What do your parents think of your profession?" she asked.

I was glancing at Mark more and more often hoping he'd interrupt this inquisition, but I only received smiles in return. His plate was empty while I had barely touched the food. My steak grew cold as I answered Ana's incessant questions. "My mother died three years ago," I said, hoping to avoid explaining about my father.

Ana's carefully coiffed white hair and small, wrinkled face gave the impression of a sweet granny. But she was sharp. "That was the last time you went home? Doesn't your father need you? You must have brothers and sisters who take care of him, no?" She nodded, apparently certain she had answered her own question. She stared straight at me and I realised who she reminded me of. Mrs Vidic had an equally disquieting habit of staring at people until they confirmed her theory or dared deny it.

"I'm an only child. And he's doing fine on his own." I had no idea if he was. I wished I had someone back home to ask about my father's situation because he stubbornly repeated the same phrase I'd just used every time I spoke to him. I thought of Walt and how his daughter asked him to move closer so she could look after him.

"Nina used to live in Paris," Mark said, now he'd

finished eating.

Ana's eyes lit up. "How was it? I think I would have loved living in Paris. It's such a charming city compared with this place."

It was clear Ana and I were complete opposites. She romanticised every place she couldn't live in and despised Melbourne, while I was most at home here.

"I can't tell you much about Paris. I spent most of my time in a restaurant kitchen," I said.

"Oh, my dear girl. How could you waste such an opportunity to experience some romance in the most magical of cities?"

A piece of steak lodged in my throat as I stared at my plate. I made a non-committal sound in response. Images of Yves flashed in front of my eyes. Ana seemed to have a radar detector for all my weakest points.

She struggled to her feet. "I'll go fetch the dessert."

Mark appeared to be watching me with interest when I lifted my eyes to his. Had he noticed my hedging when Ana mentioned romance? He raised his wine glass in a silent toast.

I dropped my knife and fork to reach for my glass. I needed the wine. "Cheers," I said, voice strangled with nerves.

"Aren't you going to finish it?" Ana said, gesturing to my half-full plate.

"I can't eat another bite." The food had already turned to rocks in my stomach. "Not if I want to try a piece of your *potica*."

Her lips formed a displeased line, but she smiled despite herself. Every Slovenian cook was most proud of their *potica* and I shamelessly used this to my benefit.

Ana cleared the plates and brought out the walnut-filled bread on a platter. "There you go," she said, pushing the platter, heaped with chunky slices, towards me.

"Thank you." I didn't look at Ana, sure of seeing disapproval in her eyes when I picked the thinnest slice.

She moved to pour me grappa she'd brought from the cupboard behind me, but I covered the glass with my hand. "I'm working later today."

She poured a glass for Mark and herself and said, "Eat, girl. I'll wrap you a piece to take home with you. You young people think it's only polite to refuse and nibble at your food like it's poisoned, instead of eating with gusto. An empty sack can't stand upright, isn't that so?"

She chuckled pleased to have hosted a fellow citizen at her traditional lunch, regardless of all my shortcomings, which she had so diligently pointed out throughout the meal.

"I'll take a piece, too," said Mark.

"You always do, my boy." She patted his hand, but when he reached for the grappa bottle to pour himself another shot, Ana moved with the grace of a ballerina and swiped it from under his nose to carry back to the cupboard.

I hid my grin behind the slice of *potica*. I would have had enough of home cooking and Slovenian hospitality for another decade by the time this lunch was finished.

That Ana let me help her load the dishes into the dishwasher must have meant I had passed her test and she regarded me as part of the family, because you didn't let strangers help clear the dining table.

In the time it took Mark and me to get from the living room to the front door, she repeated her invitation to come back three times. She held my hand in hers for a long moment, and I wouldn't have put it past her to ask me outright how serious I was about Mark. She looked so hopeful that even if she'd asked, I probably wouldn't have been able to resent it.

"It was so wonderful to have you today, Nina. *Nasvidenje*," she said instead.

"*Nasvidenje*."

The clouds were back, and halfway to the tram station, Mark and I were soaked. After the tense lunch, getting drenched in the rain must have released something in me and I laughed.

"I'm sorry about Ana," Mark said once we were on the tram. "I didn't know she'd go all Spanish Inquisition on you like that."

I was ashamed to admit I'd been used to the attitude from my childhood, so I shrugged. "It's fine. She's just looking out for you." Like Mrs Vidic had perhaps been looking out for others. Still, it was a fine line between good intentions and meddling.

"Next time, we'll go someplace where she won't be able to look out for me."

I didn't respond to the suggestion because I wasn't sure what to say. I liked Mark, not because Miren thought we'd connect over our shared roots but in spite of it. Meeting Ana had made that clear.

The ride back into the city seemed longer than fifteen minutes because the wet clothes clung to me. When the time for goodbye came, we stood awkwardly on the pavement in front of Flinders Street Station.

From how his eyes dropped to my mouth, I knew he'd kiss me. I was curious about how it would feel, but I wasn't sure I wanted him to. His lips were soft, giving me the chance to stop him. I didn't. By the time he pulled back, I thought I could get used to him kissing me.

As promised, our next two dates didn't include Ana. I still wasn't quite sure about us, though. Ten months had passed since Yves and I had broken up, but I wasn't ready yet for a new relationship. I liked how Mark did everything with a smile and an open mind. He was nice and friendly and there was nothing wrong with him, but there was plenty amiss with us. When I was with him, I felt his warmth and generosity, his physical presence. But when he wasn't with me, I thought of Yves instead. If I was uncertain in the kitchen, Yves's hot breath whispered in my ear; when my nights off became lonely and the idle days long, his fingers caressed my wrist, his eyes watched me, his skin warmed me up. When I caught a wave and rode it to the shore, I wished Yves could see me, not Mark, although he was the surfer. Even when Mark kissed me, images of Yves assaulted me sometimes. Mark couldn't compete with that. It wouldn't be fair of me to set him up to fail.

Back home, after our fifth date, when we had taken a trip to the Yarra Valley, I couldn't settle. Nervous energy propelled me out onto the balcony. Despite the clouds, the sky looked endless. There was something freeing in its vastness. The city wasn't boxed in by mountains and forbiddingly steep slopes. Its expanse was full of potential, infinite options for discoveries, for getting lost and finding oneself, for anonymity. I liked that: not being bound by obligation to others. I didn't need belonging; I needed freedom, however selfish that made me.

Mark called on a Monday afternoon in March, just as

I walked into Philippe's kitchen, about to answer the phone. I turned the volume down and let it ring in my bag. I had to sort things out in my head first.

EIGHT

I had no idea what had got into me. The idea of visiting Ana on my own had been so preposterous that at first, I didn't take it seriously. I didn't know how I had got from that to walking down the street towards her house. I didn't know if she would welcome me, but I rang the doorbell anyway.

I felt justified in being here without Mark simply because she was Slovenian. I felt a kinship with her I didn't feel with Mark despite his descent. And yet I ridiculed her for clinging to the symbols and traditions of the old country. But a secret part of me understood. It was the same as me dwelling on hurtful memories. I knew they would upset me and rekindle the ache inside, but I couldn't let them go.

Ana frowned when she opened the door, and then her face brightened in recognition.

"Am I intruding?"

"Certainly not. Come in."

"I hope you don't mind me coming alone."

"Just as well. We won't have to pretend we're Australian," Ana said in Slovenian.

Her willingness to dismiss Mark startled me, although I'd done the same thing by coming alone. Now I regretted it. Why had I chosen to visit this Slovenian enclave? Was it a sort of penance for not going home more often?

A head shorter than me, Ana strained to place her hand on my shoulder then led me into the living room with unexpected firmness. I had the feeling that her bossiness wasn't so much to do with the pleasure of playing the hostess as it was the sense that she was well-versed in being a Slovenian abroad, while I was a novice at it.

She ordered me to sit and went into the kitchen. Unlike our living room at home, this room had large windows looking onto the garden. The flames in the wood-burning stove in the corner shone bright and warm. I looked around and found myself immersed in the past. Decorative plates—just like my mother's—stared at me from the wall, the cupboard held mementos from Lake Bled and Radenci, and a dried edelweiss bowed its head to me from a shot glass. Everything was spotless. Not even the Australian dust could touch this pristine shrine to the homeland.

I didn't miss any of these things or what they represented, but they filled me with an odd sense of grief at being unable to connect with them. They had been part of me, of my childhood, but I had never been able to accept them.

What Ana didn't understand—and I had only just realised—was that the lace tablecloth, the calendar with the images of the Alps, the herbs soaking in grappa behind the glass cupboard doors were all symptoms of fear of losing oneself, of having nowhere to belong, nowhere to return. But by creating this shrine, Ana had condemned herself to not belonging here. Yet time had washed away the village of her memories. So this was all she had left: a bubble of a place and a time that no longer existed anywhere but here.

But I didn't have to belong to the past. I existed in the here and now, and I could choose the parts of my Slovenianness that were worth revisiting. Maybe that was what I was doing by trying out old recipes for Walt, choosing the ones I liked and which reflected my personality. Like the *potica* I baked that morning, but with almonds because I didn't like walnuts.

I reached for a piece of Ana's *potica* now when she placed a plate of it in front of me, together with a cup of steaming coffee.

"Do you know," she said, "I tasted my first cup of real coffee only once I came here. Back home, my mother used chicory. The real beans were too expensive for us."

"Melbourne is famous for its good coffee," I said, remembering the mouth-watering smell of roasting beans on my walk here from the tram station.

"I sometimes miss chicory." Ana sighed and clasped her hands on the table in front of her.

I struggled to hide my smile. "What did you do when you arrived in Melbourne?"

She looked at me with hesitation, as if cautioning me this might not be the story I wanted to hear.

"I arrived five years after my brother," she said, at last, sounding almost resentful. "He suggested I come, said I'd find work here and live in peace. But once I arrived, he wasn't waiting for me; he was up in the Snowy Mountains, helping build the dams. I didn't know a word of English when I set foot on Australian soil. I just wanted to die then, you know?" Her chin trembled as she stared into her cup. The memories seemed to age her already wrinkled face. If she'd stayed in Bohinj, her skin wouldn't be so tanned, perhaps not as wrinkled. Would her hands still shake when remembering her youth, though? "I wanted one of the heavy crates being unloaded from the ship to fall on me and end it."

"Didn't your brother come for you?" I asked.

She shook her head. "He stayed up there for another two years. It was 1953 when I saw him for the first time since he'd left the home country, and I didn't recognise him. I walked right past him as he was waiting for me in front of the post office in Bonegilla." She looked at me with wonder, as if she still couldn't believe she hadn't recognised her own brother. "He used to be a handsome fella, but now he was all wild. His hair long, his skin like leather. But I suppose women still found him attractive." She must have meant Mark's mother. "We didn't look anything alike anymore," she added, resentment obvious in her tone.

It was hard to tell how much of her story was fact and how much her disappointment with her new home coloured it. She made it sound as though she'd lost her brother to Australia. But from what Mark had said, emigrating to Australia was what had saved his father from the secret police. For many of those who had stayed, it didn't end well. Maybe Mark's father didn't have a choice.

"He helped me find work as a seamstress, at least," Ana said.

My empty coffee cup clanked on the metal tray. I didn't want to place it on the lace tablecloth in case I stained it. "Mark said you helped raise him. He's fond of you."

"He's a good boy," she said, her sharp eyes on me.

"Doesn't take after his father."

I was curious why she had never married but I suspected I knew. She had come here for her brother, either because he wanted her to or she wanted to be close to him. Apparently, it hadn't gone as planned. Physically, she might have emigrated to the other side of the world, but her heart stayed behind, safely tucked away amidst the mountains of her home so no Australian man could steal it.

I felt sorry for her, for her stubborn pride that had only caused her pain. Why couldn't she see that?

"Do you have any other family members left?" I asked.

She shook her head. "Just Mark's father and Mark. But he's half…"

She sighed and picked up the tray, ending the conversation. There were so many questions I still wanted to ask. Why hadn't she returned home if she hated it so much here? Wouldn't she be happier if she accepted that the Slovenia she used to know no longer existed? But I'd caused her enough distress for one day.

"Could I ask you…?" I began, but then stopped. How far did her sympathy for a fellow expat extend? Would she be willing to keep this meeting from Mark?

She looked sad when she said, "I won't say a word to Mark. But if you break his heart…"

We both knew there was nothing she could do about it, just like I couldn't make any promises after I'd already ignored his call once.

Instead of taking the tram, I walked to the restaurant to stretch my legs before I started the dinner shift. It took me an hour to get to Southbank. I rolled my neck to relieve the tension. The afternoon sun blinded me. Upbeat pop music from a bar followed me halfway down the street. It was nearly Easter, and although I had experienced my first Christmas on the beach slathered in zinc sunscreen, I still found the Easter eggs and fluffy bunnies in shop windows incongruous with the autumn colour palette.

After closing hours, the mise en place for the next day was delayed because of a storeroom mishap. It was almost five in the morning when I got home. For the first time since arriving in Melbourne, my flat felt lonely rather than peaceful. In the quiet of the apartment, my self-reproach was too loud. I hadn't been honest with Mark, nor Ana when she asked me not to break his heart. I hadn't been honest with my father for a long time now. But my thoughts also kept returning to Walt. I'd tried another one of my mother's recipes that night, in case he showed up. This one came to me more easily. I thought about how Walt had given up his life on the farm because moving to Melbourne would make his daughter feel more secure. Would my father be willing to do the same? For that matter, would I?

Restless from the rush of a busy night, it was pointless trying to sleep. My surfing gang would be on Sorrento beach in an hour, so I decided to head that way. With the light early morning traffic, I would be in the waves in less than an hour and a half.

I didn't bother attaching my board to the rack of my car. I stashed it in the back, next to the holdall with towels and a change of clothes and the esky. A smile crept up my face as I remembered my confusion when I first heard Jim mentioning his "esky", and then the realisation it was just an ordinary cooler box.

"Looky what the tide's brought in," Ida joked when I walked towards them over the dunes. I recognised her voice, but couldn't see her because the low sun was in my eyes and I could only make out two silhouettes ahead.

"What are you doing up so early?" Bart asked.

"Haven't gone to bed yet," I said.

"What are you, fifteen?" he joked.

I was still grateful to Bart and Jim for helping me when I had just started to surf. Ida had bandaged my thigh, which I had scratched on a sharp rock, and offered me a fizzy drink. Next time we met on the beach they invited me to join them. They were locals, and their knowledge about the best surfing spots was invaluable, so I joined them whenever I could. In the six months I'd known them, we'd gone from casual surfing buddies to good friends.

"Well, I've got to be in the office in an hour. I better go catch some waves. It's looking sweet out there," Bart said, grabbing his board and walking towards the waves.

The beach was deserted at this early hour, apart from a few surfers and joggers. The crisp air caused goosebumps to rise on my skin. I followed Bart with my eyes as he walked into the surf and then stumbled half a step back as a wave pummelled him. What he'd called sweet, I would call rough. The waves were high, too high for someone who only had six months of surfing under her belt. Perhaps I should wait this one out.

"Are you sure? It's not that rough," Ida said.

I didn't realise I'd spoken aloud. "Maybe, but I'm too tired to give it my all."

So when Ida joined Bart and Jim in the surf, I dropped onto the sand and pulled out Fiona Capp's memoir about her love of surfing.

A seagull's peeved cry made me look up in time to see Ida try to stand on the tip of her board and fall. The massive wave swallowed her, and it took a while for her head to bob up to the surface. The next minute, she was back on her board, paddling out to the queue, or line-up as surfers called it, waiting for a second chance.

I'd had plenty of second chances, more than I deserved, probably. They led me here, to Sorrento back beach with basalt bluffs to my right and chilly golden sand under my feet, so I must have used them well. Paris-trained Slovenian living the quintessential Australian life. I had nothing to complain about. So why did I feel so unsettled? There was something missing, something that frustrated me with its elusiveness.

Although it was March, the sun still had a sting in it as I returned to my car mid-morning. Once the wind had abated, I'd paddled out to the line-up and caught a few waves, so my trip to the peninsula hadn't been in vain.

It took me more than two hours to get back to the city. With my adrenaline draining, I felt sluggish from the lack of sleep and the warm sun through the windscreen.

I almost stopped the car in the middle of the street when I saw Mark outside my apartment door. Parallel parking was an effort when my attention kept returning to the intruder. What would I say to him? I took my time getting out of the car. I was trying so hard to gauge Mark's expression from the corner of my eye that I bumped my head on the boot hatch and nearly dropped my bag. I felt anxious inviting him in, but he took hold of the esky to take it inside, and I couldn't prevent him from coming in without being rude.

I hadn't slept in twenty-four hours, and the late shift and surfing had sapped my energy. My mind was fuzzy. Seeing Mark's mild expression and his readiness to help after I'd ignored his calls added to the confusion. I unlocked the front door on my second attempt. Kicking off my flip-flops, I dropped my purse and keys on the kitchen table. I turned to tell Mark where to put the esky, but he wasn't there. "Mark?"

He was standing at the door, the esky dangling in his hand like a weight on a balance scale.

"Aren't you going to come in?"

"May I?" His smile was tentative, almost apologetic, as if he knew how much I wished I could postpone this.

I gestured with my head towards the kitchen and then took the esky from him when he came in.

He walked to the window while I washed my hands and put on a pot to brew coffee.

"So, obviously you've been avoiding me." He looked down at his hands. His jeans hung low on his waist and his creased t-shirt made him look vulnerable. "I figured I might try to convince you to give me another chance."

It didn't seem fair to upset such a nice person, but the thought of a serious relationship, with him or anyone, made me claustrophobic. I couldn't envisage it going anywhere. Because I didn't want it to. Would I get married? Have children? There was no place for that in my life or heart. Ana was right. My profession didn't allow much time for anything else. And then there was Yves and the still vivid, painful memories. He was still part of my life, even thousands of kilometres and a break-up away.

When Mark turned to look at me with that same

uncertain smile as before, I blurted, "I've been to see Ana." It was clear this was not what he had expected. "I went on my own. I shouldn't have; she's your aunt. I thought…" I stopped mid-sentence. He stared at me, and I felt like a fool. "I hoped…"

"I understand," he said, fully turning to me now. "She's lived here for decades, and she knows what it's like to leave your home country. I knew you'd bond over it when I suggested you visit her with me."

I hadn't visited her so she would help me cope with my move here. I'd gone to see her because although we were different, we had some things in common and I thought it might help me understand why I couldn't settle. But I was just as confused as before.

"In any case, that's not why you're here," I said, too tired to explain it to him.

"No."

"Mark." He opened his mouth to say something, but I stopped him with my raised hand. "You need to know something… I ended a relationship just before I came here. I'm not… I'm not fully over it yet."

"Do you still love him?"

I usually liked how direct Mark was, but it could also be terribly inconvenient.

"It's not just about the relationship. I worked with Yves for a year, and before that he was my instructor at the cookery school, so you see…" I tried to explain but my words didn't adequately express how I felt, how interconnected it all was for me: cooking, love, grief, life.

"And you're having problems forgetting him?" Mark came closer. I'd known him for almost two months. Even if we weren't a real couple, we were friendly. Him entering my personal space shouldn't feel so intrusive. "I get it," he said. "All I'm asking is for you to give me a chance. I really like you."

I'd run out of reasonable excuses. Mark was a decent man and maybe my best chance to get over the break-up with Yves, but I couldn't answer.

"Go out with me this Sunday," he urged. "There's a comedy night on at a local brewery. Pizza, beer, and some laughs is all I'm asking."

The smart thing to do would be to tell him I'd think about it and then get a few hours' sleep. But the fact he remembered I had Sunday evenings off touched me. His hand on my cheek was so gentle.

I nodded and I felt better when his face lit up. "When was the last time you had any sleep?" he asked after a pause. Before I could answer, he gave me a peck on the cheek. His hand slid in a soft caress down my still-damp hair. "Goodnight."

I welcomed most changes in my life in Melbourne. Still, it seemed that the more at home I felt here, the more I thought of and missed my home country. I couldn't get Ana's story of her coming here out of my mind. How lonely she must have felt when she hadn't recognised her own brother. Had she felt betrayed by him when he'd so quickly become too Australian for her Slovenian soul?

All this going in circles confused me; I wanted to avoid the growing homesickness. So I kept busy at Philippe's. We were always full because we were popular with the locals as well as tourists. On my mornings off, I surfed, explored the city, or lounged on the beach, until autumn chased me away from the April streets and into the cosy shelter of my apartment.

Mark and I went to that comedy night, but after, I kissed him on my doorstep and went up to my flat alone. His company was easy and comfortable, and I enjoyed my time with him, but I couldn't quite bring myself to let him in. He called the next day and asked if I wanted to visit Ana again, but I said no. Perhaps he thought if I connected with her, I would find it easier to welcome him into my life, too. But the foreign wind Ana brought with her was bound to ruffle my calm and only complicate things further. She'd already sneaked her way into my dreams: one night, I had woken covered in sweat from a dream in which I was cooking a meal for her in my childhood home under my mother's supervision.

I kept thinking about what I wanted from Mark. It wasn't fair to string him along with false promises if I wasn't willing to commit. I was torn between liking Mark and longing for Yves, between needing calm in my life and wanting the whirlwind passion I'd experienced in Paris.

This indecision wouldn't let me sleep and I often ended up going to work early. One such sleepy autumn morning, as Jeff poured me a coffee, he said, "You've been coming in at dawn lately; I have to start the coffee machine extra early just for you. Why do you want the coffee piping hot? You can't drink it like that, anyhow."

"I want to have the choice of how I drink it."

Jeff's wild looks were deceptive. Maybe that was his way of catching people unprepared, his edge. He'd married right out of vocational school, he'd told me on my second day at the bistro. His three children went to bed at nine, had lunch at one o'clock on the dot and were allowed one special toy each; the rest they had to share. His approach to parenting was no-nonsense but fair and loving. His approach to work was the same; he had rules, and the rest was all jokes and laughter. I loved working with him; he was a great person to be around.

He nodded and put the cup in front of me on the bar. "Like what you said about Melbourne being a port, a harbour, but also a way out into the world so you can either stay or leave?"

I was surprised he remembered the conversation from months before. "Yes."

"That never occurred to me, but I see your point. Escape route and all that. Are you afraid of something? Like, someone after you? A vindictive ex?" He kept busy wiping glasses, but he was watching me closely.

It was too early for such discussions, but because he seemed worried, I owed him a proper answer. "No one's after me. And it's not about fear. It's more that I have this restless feeling. There comes a time when I get an itch to leave. It's not even about whether I'm running from or towards something. I just can't settle."

"Do you think it'll stop? That you'll stop?" He frowned as he looked at me.

"I'm beginning to hope so."

"That's a start. You need an anchor."

There were voices at the door outside, although the bistro wasn't open yet.

"I thought—" I started, and then Philippe's voice said behind me, "Nina, look who's here."

I turned and stiffened. Yves stood next to my boss, tall, arresting, unshaven.

Philippe glanced from me to Yves and back. Yves's eyes were on me. He looked so reassuringly familiar, yet somehow different. My mouth was dry.

"Recognise him?" Philippe chuckled, slapping Yves's back. "He's got old."

I lowered myself from the bar stool and walked towards Yves, as if I couldn't entirely control my limbs and something in him compelled me to go to him.

"*Salut*," he murmured.

I couldn't speak. He kissed my cheeks. His stubble scratched away another layer of my composure. My face was simultaneously hot and cold under the scrutiny of the three men.

I felt somehow closed off from the scene, distanced. I remembered years before—a lifetime ago, it seemed—I had driven from Stockholm to Linköping in the middle of winter. On the way, I noticed boarded-up stalls by the side of the road, mostly in the middle of nowhere. Ståle told me those were produce stalls where people sold cherries and strawberries during the summer months. That was how I felt now. Boarded up against the intrusion of this trans-Pacific breeze.

At the first opportunity, I snuck to the kitchen. I cleaned the storage room, leaving Miren aghast, and started on mise en place without a coffee break, surprising even myself. I refused to think about Yves talking with Philippe metres away, but even so, I trembled with anticipation and anxiety. What was he doing here? What would I say to him? Why hadn't Philippe told me Yves was coming? I vacillated between resentment, elation, and nerves.

Yves stayed with Philippe the entire morning. Did that mean he hadn't missed me like I'd missed him? A vicious headache crept up my neck and into my temples, where it pounded to the rhythm of my heartbeat. There was so much I wanted to say to him, but I couldn't find the words as confused emotions liquefied my insides.

During service, I was distracted. Miren kept fixing my blunders, exchanging confused glances with Jeff more than once. I didn't comment. After lunch, Yves left with Philippe, looking at me with what I thought was regret.

The memory of that look still haunted me when my phone rang later. My chest squeezed as I saw Mark's name on the display. I was about to answer it and tell him about my torn feelings, how I couldn't be with him because a part of me would always reject him, reject us. But ending it over the phone felt crass and unkind. So I let it ring.

The next morning, Yves gave a short presentation to the kitchen staff. It was a Monday, when the bistro was closed to the public.

He stood still and tall next to Philippe. Even with a sleepless night and nervousness making my throat tight, treacherous warmth swelled in my chest. I was tempted to give in.

"*Salut*, Nina," Yves had said when I entered the kitchen. I was grateful for the presence of the others so I could avoid talking to him alone for a little longer. I was glad he didn't use his nickname for me. Just seeing him after almost a year was hard enough.

Philippe introduced him as a friend from Paris visiting to give us inspiration. Jeff nodded his appreciation, while Miren openly assessed Yves, glancing at me from time to time until I worried my face would betray my emotions.

"Yves will prepare a dessert; he got the idea for it on the aeroplane here," Philippe said. "So bear in mind that he will prepare it for the first time. No testing beforehand. The kitchen is yours, *mon ami*."

Yves didn't so much as look my way, but that was how he cooked. To most people, food was essential for survival, but to Yves it was sustenance on an entirely different level. There was something broken in how he found more satisfaction and solace in pots and appliances than people. But was I any different? I was only too ready to lose myself in cooking, so long as I didn't have to think and remember.

Everyone in the kitchen got a serving of the chocolate panna cotta and rosemary ice cream, but when it was time for me to get mine, he ran out of panna cotta. He motioned for me to come closer. I went because I suspected this had been his plan from the beginning. That I knew him so well was gratifying, but it also hurt because it reminded me of what we'd once had.

He spooned some panna cotta from his plate, adding the ice cream, slowly, almost sensuously, before offering it to me. A drop of the ice cream ended up on my chin. The chocolate and rosemary flavours blended in harmony in my mouth.

All my senses were on high alert, trying to decipher and memorise the tastes and nuances, but it didn't escape my notice that he had wiped the drop from my chin with his thumb.

I cleared my throat. I hadn't expected to ever see Yves again and to now be standing so close I could smell his aftershave robbed me of speech.

His dark eyes bored into me. "Philippe tells me you've settled in nicely."

I wanted to explain, but telling him I liked this new life

felt like treason after our two years together. I had no words to elaborate on why I preferred Melbourne to Paris or how that didn't stop me from, and maybe made me even more susceptible to, often remembering the life we'd shared. Perhaps I didn't feel at home in Melbourne because of the city but because of me and how I'd changed.

"You don't miss Paris?" Yves asked.

I shook my head and froze. Was he really talking about Paris? "A bit. Perhaps."

He smiled knowingly. It was almost like old times.

"So what do you think?" he asked.

"About Paris?"

"The dessert?" He pointed to the empty plate. I couldn't remember eating all of it.

"It's good."

"Good?" he repeated, his expression vacillating between incredulity and annoyance.

"Yes, well, better than good." I fumbled with words as I did every time he quizzed me about food. Some things didn't change even when you moved to the other side of the world.

"You disappoint me, Ninotchka." He shook his head. "Your food vocabulary is still lacking, even after all these years and despite all my tutoring."

The excitement of Yves's presence hardened into a rock in the pit of my stomach. I felt as insecure and ignorant as the first day at the cookery school. I thought I'd outgrown being a disappointment to him. But maybe this wasn't about me being found lacking. Maybe he was still lashing out, as Thoma had said, trying to restore his power over me. Maybe this was his childish way of coping with being hurt after I chose to work for Philippe.

Yves and Philippe left soon after. I heard them chatting in the alley outside, probably sharing a smoke.

I took my cardigan off the hook in my locker.

"Cheerio," I said to Jeff, who was setting tables for breakfast the next morning.

"Just a bit longer and you'll be ours." He grinned from above a stack of table napkins.

I stopped mid-stride. "Excuse me?"

"You're beginning to talk like us, love," Jeff said.

"No, I'm not."

"Uh-hum." He was hunched over the table he was setting.

"I am?"

He looked exasperated at me. "Would I lie to you?"

I smiled. "Yes, you would."

"Yeah, okay, I would. But I'm not lying about this."

"Ta."

I opened the door and then stopped. Philippe and Yves were getting into Philippe's car. Yves turned and looked at me over its roof. I couldn't tear my eyes from him. He smiled, ducked his head, and got into the car.

Then to my dismay, I saw Mark standing by the door, a witness to my silent exchange with Yves.

"Hey," he said.

I winced. I'd left him a message that I had to work on my day off, and I had hoped it would give me at least a few days to find the right words to explain things.

Mark seemed quiet, the skin around his mouth grey, as if he was unwell.

"Hello," I said, but he stared at the car.

The engine revved and Philippe's blue Audi drove

away. Mark looked at me. "So that's Yves." I struggled for words to make this less painful. But Mark's face already said everything I couldn't. "I'm not going to stick around. There are only so many blows my pride can take," he said, sounding almost untroubled, as if he believed I'd buy his act. I hated that he thought so little of me. "Goodbye, Nina."

He turned his back on me so suddenly I was caught unawares. "Mark?" He stopped, but a long moment passed before he turned back. "I'm sorry," I said.

His face was a kaleidoscope of emotions, twisted with hurt, lips a tight line, but then a ghost of a smile touched his eyes. "Not your fault."

He was generous even now, something I never seemed capable of. Because I knew the mess was my fault.

The alley was cast in shadows and Mark's tall, dark silhouette blended into the surroundings as if he had never been there. The swiftness with which he vanished filled me with an air of finality. Another path not taken; another door closed. I was repeating the same mistake. Only, a mistake repeated a second time wasn't a mistake. It was a choice.

When Yves showed up at my door the next evening, it was easy to slip back into my old life, as if I hadn't left Paris a year before, as if I hadn't said goodbye to Mark the day before. If I hadn't known better, I'd have thought this—being with Yves, there and then—was how home felt.

Jeff once told me that we didn't remember people and events—we remembered what we felt when we met or experienced them. Emotions made memories vivid and lasting. It was why we remembered the taste of our favourite childhood dish long into old age. It was why we recognised a lover's smell in a crowd on a busy street.

In the dim light of the two candles by my bed, it was impossible to see Yves's features clearly, and yet I did. Everything was familiar, as if, along the way, they had become part of me: his body next to mine in the sheets, his breath in my ear. He whispered to me in French, and though I didn't understand, I sensed the words in their visceral, non-verbal sense. He uttered them with a passion eclipsing their individual meanings. I had missed Yves but I only now realised how much.

"How are things at the restaurant?" I asked.

I didn't mind when, instead of answering, he responded with questions of his own. "Melbourne seems a nice city to stay in, *non*? Is Philippe good to you?"

I made a sound of agreement. "What's your latest class like?" I asked. "As ignorant as we were?" He muted my chuckle with his mouth.

We talked to hear each other's voices. We weren't interested in answers. We only ever truly communicated with our bodies and cooking. I used to think it was because the language we shared was foreign to us both. Sometimes words didn't come when you needed them. But then I thought of the many times I had the words ready but held them back because I wasn't sure what his response would be. I wished that could change, but with me in Melbourne and him in Paris, the timing was never right. Or perhaps our intentions weren't.

The days rushed by and I was afraid to ask Yves what would happen once his two weeks in Melbourne were over. I cooked to keep the anxiety in check.

Two days before he was due to fly back to France, I invited him over and served him plum dumplings in a sauce of butter, wine, crème fraiche, and breadcrumbs. My mother's version of the dish had been simpler, but perhaps spiced with homesickness, I remembered it being tastier. We ate at the table for two on my balcony, and I was taken aback to realise that because Walt had never shown up at the bistro, Yves was the first person to taste one of my dishes based on my mother's recipes. I leaned back in my chair, surprised by the knowledge, but pleased. Perhaps this was happiness.

The setting sun laid golden leaves on the surface of the sea below. The city was deep in autumn, but after a satisfying summer when we had just enough of everything and not too much of anything, we welcomed it.

Yves concentrated on the food and didn't speak for a long time. The past two weeks of sunshine had left cinnamon freckles on his pale skin. I loved how familiar he was, yet I kept discovering new things about him, like his freckled skin. Or the detail on his upper arm tattoo, which I had only realised last night was an image of wings. Or how, when he smiled now, his smile reached his eyes and they creased with warmth. But that had all been there all along; it was I who saw things differently; I had changed. I'd known him for almost three years and I only now realised how deeply I loved him. Yet I could not envisage a happy ending for us.

"You've outdone yourself, Nina," Yves said, a pensive smile on his lips. He watched me, and I couldn't interpret his expression. "You've found your place."

"I don't know."

Yves's words reminded me of Mark. Mark could have

been "my place". I missed his voice, even his unabashed laugh, and I regretted losing the simplicity he would have brought into my life. But as I sat across from Yves, the feasibility of a relationship with Mark was as thin as dreams. Mark was wholesome, friendly, and uncomplicated, but Yves was everything else.

"I said you would."

"No, you didn't."

"I thought it, then." He ate another forkful of the dessert. "Why else do you think I was so hard on you?"

I had never thought he had ulterior motives for his behaviour or that his brusqueness wasn't just who he was. "Why else do you think I let you go, back in Paris?" His voice was uncharacteristically tense.

"Let me go?" Whatever he was trying to say differed so much from how I had seen things that, for a moment, I thought we were talking about two unrelated events.

"You needed to find your place. Without me in it."

Even if that were true, he needn't have sacrificed our relationship for it. "You could have been less arrogant and asked my opinion," I said.

He leaned back in his chair, a curious expression on his face. "Would you have left if I'd asked you not to?" he asked, eyebrows raised.

No, I wouldn't have. He knew me well enough to know that. I wouldn't have come to Melbourne. I'd have missed out on the chance to create and explore, and lead my own team. Much smaller than the one I had been part of in Paris, but mine. He was right; I had found my place. Thanks to him. And just like that, my anger was doused.

I leaned back, out of the bubble of our conversation. Where were we headed? What did all this coming together and breaking apart mean? I was familiar with feeling lost, but it wasn't something I associated with Yves. There was always a purpose to everything he did. He even ate like that, with gusto, as though the essence of food mattered and not just its carefully planned and detailed preparation.

Later, he made love the same way. His mouth tasted and nibbled while his skin warmed me in the oncoming dusk. Being with him was like licking the last drops of the heady wine sauce, the traces of alcohol spreading through my veins, fragile with the lack of lovemaking over the past few months.

Through the waves of the curtain fabric, the calm of the evening settled on our naked bodies, cooling us.

My fingers trailed over Yves's warm stomach. "How did you know where I lived?" That first night when I had opened the door to find him standing on the landing, it hadn't occurred to me to ask him how he'd found me.

"Philippe told me."

"Why?"

"I asked."

"Why?" My fingers traced patterns on his skin and through his black hairs and occasional grey ones. Unlike before, in Paris, I wasn't afraid of his terseness. I wanted to know why he had come here, sought me out. I wanted him to tell me, and above all, to admit it to himself. It was time we defined us, what we were to each other, what we were together.

"Ninotchka, stop, please." He kissed me, to silence me, I suspected. He tasted sharp on my tongue, the flavour of a full-bodied red wine with earthy undertones, aged in oak barrels.

"Why?" I insisted.

"Enough with the whys! Why, why, why! Is that all you can say? *Merde!*"

"It's just a question, Yves."

"No, not just a question. There are too many questions!" He raked his too long hair. The bed dipped as he got up.

He dressed quickly, his back turned to me.

"Yves?" I hadn't wanted to upset him but it hurt that he was never willing to give me anything. Our relationship had never reached the point where we could be generous. Perhaps we had been the closest to that in our final days in Paris, but then Philippe had appeared. "I just wanted—" I started.

"I wanted to see you, that's all," he interrupted, shrugging.

"Why is that so hard for you to say? Doesn't this mean anything?" I pointed between us. "Anything at all?" Wrapped in the crumpled sheet, I got out of bed. As I stood in front of him, it felt wrong that he was only a few centimetres taller than me. He had always seemed towering, despite my height. "What am I to you?" I asked. There were words I wanted—needed—to hear from him. I knew he cared, but his reluctance to admit that upset me.

"Why are you making this so difficult?" His pouting lips made him look like a spoiled child, ridiculous and unreasonable.

"I'm not. But I feel used, Yves, and I hate that."

When I had seen him in Philippe's kitchen on his first morning in Melbourne, when I saw that he had missed me too, I was overwhelmed by hope and relief. It made me realise I had been so unsettled the past few months because something was missing. Nothing I'd felt in my friendships with Miren and Jeff, or even with Mark, had been as strong and vital as what I had shared with Yves in Paris. I had thought we could rekindle that. I had thought he wanted it, too.

I had planned things to show Yves in Melbourne. I thought of taking him to the beach. I hoped to teach him to surf or take a couple of days off and take him on a road trip up to Sydney. But I'd planned too far ahead. We would never go on road trips, wearing sunglasses and hats, laughing at nothing and everything. We only existed as a couple in a rumpled bed lit by a pair of taper candles in empty wine bottles.

"You're being melodramatic," he whispered, his face turning red and then green from the traffic light on the street.

"If that were so, I'd have thrown you out after the first two times in Paris." My bruised soul didn't have the energy for anger any more. "I understand you're not very good at expressing your emotions. But I deserve better, Yves, and you can't even tell me why you're here. What do you want from me? Am I just holiday entertainment? Do you care about me at all?" I hated how my voice broke. I hated how it was now clear this would never work. He was silent. I told him, "Please go."

"Nina?"

I turned away.

His jacket rustled as he picked it up from the chair. In the short silence that followed, I wondered if the room was holding its breath, too, anticipating his next words.

"*Tu m'as manqué, voilà pourquoi.* I missed you so much my cooking became crap."

My whole body trembled at the raw note in his voice,

but I couldn't turn around. I could not make myself vulnerable to him again. Being with Yves drained me. He was too demanding and gave too little in return. And even if he'd missed me, he wouldn't stay in Melbourne.

His soft footsteps on the hardwood floor died as the door closed behind him. His words seemed to ricochet off the walls. But then even the echo was gone, and I realised what I'd done, the finality of it.

I was only half lucid in the kitchen the next day. Miren tried talking to me, but I avoided her. I struggled to keep my tears at bay when Philippe left in the late afternoon to share a farewell drink with Yves before he went to the airport. By the time I fell into bed at midnight, Yves was halfway across the Pacific. I was heartbroken, again.

All my relationships had been as fragile as a reflection on a calm surface, to be shattered irreparably by the tiniest pebbles. I was always the one who threw the first stone.

Over the next weeks, I picked up my phone to call him more times than I wished to admit. I quizzed Philippe, as subtly as I could, but he either didn't know or wouldn't say anything about how Yves was. I worked double shifts when Miren fell ill, but even the additional work didn't keep me busy enough to stop my thoughts. One minute, I regretted letting Yves go, the next, I would tell myself it had been the right thing. The only thing to do, really. Then I would repeat the process all over, wiping my tears before my co-workers noticed them.

By the end of June, two months after Yves left, I was exhausted from missing him. It had left me feeling unwell for weeks. Emotional as I was, I thought about my father often, wondering how he was. I even thought of Walt and how, if he ever came to the bistro, I would tell him I'd enjoyed revisiting my mother's recipes for the first time in years. I spent every spare moment cooking, concocting new dishes and modifying old ones, just to keep busy. But I couldn't avoid questioning my fondness for Walt. Bonding with strangers I met in cafés was not something I had done before. But there was something about Walt, his vulnerability and loneliness, which made me feel for him. I kept thinking about how he'd moved closer to his daughter, leaving behind his home just so she wouldn't have to worry about him being alone. I thought of my father living alone, perhaps waiting endlessly for me to call. Maybe I wanted Walt to come to the bistro so much because he was a sort of substitute father. I needed him so I could express my long-suppressed daughterly feelings. But Walt never showed up.

Miren wasn't the only one to fall ill. Over the past month, half the staff had called in with the flu at one point or another, and one cold and wet July night, after I'd phoned for a taxi to get home, I sat shivering on the back seat.

"This weekend is supposed to see the lowest temperatures in years," the driver said, glancing over his shoulder. He must have seen my shaking because he tapped the display and the next moment heat blasted from the vents. I had to move my knee so it wouldn't get burnt, but I still couldn't stop the trembling. I must have caught the flu, too.

Once home, I burrowed under the covers, dressed in two jumpers, tracksuit bottoms, and woollen socks. The red light from the digits on the alarm clock cut through the darkness of the room. It was nearing one in the morning. I closed my eyes to shut it out.

When I woke, it took me a few moments to establish the source of the noise, and then a few more to find my ringing phone. The clock showed it was ten past two. It was an odd hour for a phone call. For a heart-stopping moment, when I saw it wasn't a national call, I hoped it was Yves.

"Hello?" I said, my voice shrill. I turned the light on and then shut my eyes when it blinded me.

"Ms Švagelj? I'm calling from the hospital," someone said on the other end.

The voice wasn't Yves's. A long moment passed before I realised the language wasn't English either, but Slovenian.

"I'm sorry to inform you that your father has been admitted to hospital," the male voice continued. "He's had several seizures in the past few days."

"Is he alright? I've been meaning to call him… I just haven't found the time yet." I fumbled for words.

"We'll do some tests in the morning," the doctor said, "but the tumour is growing faster than we thought."

"Tumour?" My throat seized up.

The line went silent for a moment. "You didn't know?" the doctor asked, at last, and I felt so stupid. I should have known; I was his daughter.

"I apologise for surprising you like this. Your father asked us to contact you." He explained the situation and I stuttered a thank you and promised to come as soon as possible.

Dazed, I went online and booked the last seat on the morning flight to Venice. Only then did I think to call Philippe and leave a message asking for a few days off. My thoughts were tangled and I babbled, and once I disconnected, I wasn't sure if I had made enough sense for him to know what had happened and why I wouldn't be coming in to work. I hesitated over calling Miren. I hated waking her up, but I'd composed myself enough by then to be coherent. If my message to Philippe had been a jumbled mess, she might help clear things up in the morning.

She grunted into the phone after the sixth ring.

"Sorry to wake you, Ren. I just wanted to tell you I need to go home."

"What? Who's this?" Her voice became sharper, less woolly.

"It's Nina. My father's in hospital. I'm flying home in the morning."

I heard rustling on the line as she sat up in bed. "Oh. Do you need anything? How can I help?"

"Thanks, I'm okay. Just tell Philippe, please."

"Of course. Take your time, don't rush back."

In my mind, I was already going through the things I needed to pack. I decided not to take more than a week's supply of clothes.

When I disconnected and then opened the suitcase on my bed, it finally struck me. I was going home.

NINE

The third time I visit my father, he's more lucid.

"I'm sorry, Nina," he says, almost as soon as I sit by his bed. His eyes look livelier than I have seen them in a while. More remorseful, too.

"For what?"

"Everything. For growing so distant." His Adam's apple bobs as he swallows, and it looks painful. "For not being a better father to you."

Saying he was a good father would be a lie, and he would recognise it as such. So I stay silent and place my hand on top of his on the cover. I squeeze his bony fingers as tears fill my eyes.

The noise of a squeaky wheelchair and people talking in the hallway penetrates the quiet room, making it feel both isolated and connected to the outside world. I wish I were anywhere else, yet I would never forgive myself if I hadn't come.

I clear my throat. "Things were, well, complicated."

He shakes his head gently, like a dance move. "They shouldn't have been."

I think about the fights, resentment, and animosity. What was behind all that? What caused it? "You could be so mean to Mother," I say. I can't look at him. It hurts to say it. I've always been a coward when it comes to talking about painful, unpleasant things. It's so much safer to say nothing, to keep them locked up.

His whole body trembles with a sob underneath the thick sheet.

I feel the need to comfort him. "But you were never mean to me."

"You were my daughter." He clears his throat before continuing, "She wouldn't let me forget that."

"Shh." I pat his hand. It looks like a hawk's claw now, but when my legs were too short to reach the swing, those hands lifted me up and sat me on it. He caught me when I nearly tumbled into the river while searching for plants to put into my herbarium for school. Now, as he holds his half-empty glass, the water sloshes over the rim.

"Are you happy?" he asks, and a moment later his face crumples.

A sob rises from my chest as I think of Yves, as I look again at my father's shrivelled hands. I think of the draughty cracks in the windows of my childhood home, the suitcase I dragged from the bus stop days before, only half full of clothes but crammed with painful memories. But then I also think of how I used to help my mother cook and I'd catch her smiling face through the steam rising out of the pots and how she'd praise me whenever I learned a new skill. I think of the patrons in Melbourne who keep coming back to the bistro because of my food. Of how Yves was willing to share his knowledge with me and how cooking connected us.

I smile, the tears slip out of the corners of my eyes. "I'm not unhappy."

My father snivels and shakes his head, tears leaving traces on his parchment skin. "But…"

The door bursts open and the noise pushes in as my father's roommate enters. One of his hands is holding a newspaper, the other pulls his drip stand. He nods in greeting and shuffles to the open window, closing it with commotion and muttering. His glance at me is a silent accusation. I wanted to let some air into the room. His obsession with draughts makes me sad. To have one's world diminish so much you only have control over whether the window is open or closed seems so hopeless.

After another hour, spent mostly in silence, my father falls into a restless sleep. His head twitches on the pillow and his hands jerk. If only I could do something to ease his mind, but I can't when I don't know the memories that chase him in his dreams. He wouldn't tell me even if I asked.

I watch him sleep and think of all the moments with him I missed.

I can't remember the last time I was ill. That is why the exhaustion, loss of weight, and upset stomach I've suffered for weeks are starting to worry me. I know it's probably just stress because of Yves and maybe the lingering virus my co-workers had and then my father ending up in hospital, but at the back of my mind, the shadows of my parents' illnesses lurk. I decide it can't hurt to see a doctor.

The waiting room is sunlit and crowded. A girl of about four is wailing in her mother's lap and the woman next to me repeatedly blows her nose. The exposure to viruses and germs almost makes me leave.

"Nina Švagelj?" the nurse calls from the door.

"That's me." I stumble up from the hard plastic seat, numb from the forty-minute wait for my appointment.

The cross-eyed giant with a lush head of dark hair who acts as the local doctor listens as I explain my symptoms. "I've been having problems with my stomach for weeks and I've lost four kilos." I can't help feeling silly, complaining about losing weight and being tired when there's an old woman in the waiting room so emaciated and old her son had to prop her up so she wouldn't slither off her seat. "I don't sleep well, I feel exhausted. I've missed my period this month and even the previous month it was barely there and late."

The doctor nods and makes notes. He has me sit on the examination table and gets his stethoscope ready.

"Do you feel stressed or depressed, unhappy maybe? More emotional than usual?" he asks, watching me with his dark eyes. After the unpleasantness of the waiting room, his kindness is disarming.

My cheeks warm and I stumble over words when I admit, "I've just ended a relationship. Well, it was three months ago. But it was... difficult."

"I see." He listens to my heart and lungs briefly. "What type of birth control were you using, if any?"

The pill used to give me headaches, so I stopped years ago. "Condoms," I say, although I'm not sure how this is relevant. "Why?"

"Oral contraceptives can affect your mood."

I'm sent to the laboratory afterwards for blood tests. I pace the laboratory waiting room and my stomach grumbles from hunger in spite of the acid storm raging in it.

Back in the doctor's office, pain shoots through my lower back as I drop into the chair.

All the doctor says when he peers at the slips is, "Aha."

It isn't even an "Aha!" that would mean he has gleaned a diagnosis from the blood work. The soft and cautious "aha" annoys me with its elusiveness.

He turns the slips, reads more, peering at me over the black rim of his glasses which reflect his computer screen. "You said you've been feeling tired recently?"

I nod.

"Any back pain or pain in your joints?"

"Yes."

With each question he looks at me and then back at the papers. The repeated motion makes it look as though he's nodding. It bothers me that he won't say what it is that he's agreeing with.

"Increased appetite?"

"But I also have trouble keeping food down." My leg bounces nervously and I try to stop it, but the second my focus returns to the doctor, the jiggling starts again.

"It's what I suspected," he says, at last. "I had your blood checked for hCG hormone." I'm about to ask what that is, when he smiles kindly and says, "You're pregnant."

"Pregnant?" I swallow. "But we used…"

"It happens more often than you think," the doctor says.

In this most unfortunate moment, I remember Yves laughing at me for saying "*préservatif*" when I meant food preservatives. I remember how we parted in Melbourne. And long before that, when we talked about Thoma proposing to Irene, how I said, "You work hard at a relationship and then it falls through like a rotten floorboard. And your foot gets stuck in the hole because you have a child that you then bounce back and forth." How Yves said, "*Tu m'as manqué, voilà pourquoi*", and I understood despite my rudimentary French.

The words all scramble into a muddle of emotions. I don't move on the chair, but the office sways. The doctor is still smiling but his comforting demeanour flows past me. For a moment, it's as if I've left my body and there's just my shell sitting there while I'm somewhere else, in a different dimension.

"Would you like a glass of water?" the doctor asks.

His voice sounds as if it's coming from far away. But his words bring me back to the present, and I shake my head. "I don't know what to say." I pick at the hem of my skirt, embarrassed to have been caught so unaware. How many women in their late twenties conceive by mistake? What must this kind, taciturn doctor think of me being so clueless, so naïve?

"I realise this is a difficult situation for you, considering the relationship is over," he says. "But I suggest you ask the nurse to schedule an appointment with the gynaecologist as soon as possible."

I walk out the door, dazed. The nurse calls the gynaecologist's office, and all the while the word "pregnant" swirls through my mind like a refrain. It's just a word and I'm unable to fully link it with its meaning. Because I can't be pregnant. We used condoms and I'm losing weight, not gaining it. There's no place in my life for a baby. Yves can't even deal with me, much less with an unplanned child. Only... he never said that, did he? He never said he didn't want children. I was the one who insisted on birth control. It was something I wouldn't let myself be careless about. So this whole mess isn't even possible with all that protection.

But the blood work says otherwise. What am I going

to do with a child on my own? I can't remember the last time I interacted with children. Their honesty and directness frighten me. I don't know how to respond to them. How can I raise one? I can't keep this baby. I don't know the first thing about babies.

"Would twenty-ninth of August at ten in the morning work for you?" the nurse asks.

I stare at her. "Yes. Yes, that's fine."

She plops the handset onto her desk and hands me a piece of paper with the date and time written on it. I hesitate, then take it.

When I don't move, she smiles softly. "You'll be all right," she says.

I want to believe her. But how am I going to be a mother when I don't even know how to be a daughter?

The ground underneath my feet is slipping like scree. Each choice I've made I thought was for the best. But all together, they've brought me here. My map must have been turned upside down; I must have set out from the wrong starting point. The worst thing is I have no idea which way to go now.

Yves said all my moving, the hiding behind foreign languages, the refusal to connect with anyone anywhere has been about me running away. The realisation of how right he is sends a chill down my spine. When things with Yves got too rough, I boarded a plane rather than confront him. I preferred to have my heart broken than admit my feelings. Even before that, I had abandoned this place, leaving my parents. I wasn't strong enough to clean the wounds and patch them up. I let them fester until they called for attention again and brought me right back where I am now trapped with all these new problems. This time, I have nowhere to run.

Drained and more than a little scared, I try to get rest on my makeshift bed on the guest room couch. But it doesn't support my back comfortably enough when I toss and turn. Perhaps it is time to move to a bedroom upstairs.

I arrived with the intention of returning to Melbourne as soon as possible. I wonder what it might mean if I stay a little longer. Maybe then I will be able to close the door behind me without remorse or guilt. But this is a house with many doors that keep opening. Locking them seems like something I could come to regret.

At last, exhausted, I manage a few hours of dreamless sleep. A clap of thunder wakes me. I check my watch. It's six in the morning.

I sip water at the kitchen window, waiting for the storm to unleash its wrath. My father asked me to water the garden. There has been no proper rain in weeks. I fleetingly remembered his request once or twice, but postponed it until later and then forgot. The dry ochre garden reminds me of the scorched Australian landscape. But the two countries have nothing in common; the similarity is an anomaly.

To clear my head I go for a walk along the river. The water level is lower than usual because of the drought. The heat and low oxygen levels have caused the algae to thrive and change the colour of the river from icy emerald to grass green. Still, it bustles over the stones as it used to. Vivacious and unstoppable, the noise is loud and constant enough to become a new sort of silence.

I hug my arms around my still flat belly. The parasite in me is taking over my body, which is trying to get rid of it. The fresh air and the rhythm of the river reverberating through the valley help settle my stomach.

The wide landscape of loneliness in me craves someone's closeness. But my father is slipping from my grasp faster than the river rushes by and I have no one else. Except Yves… His intense personality makes him tactless and critical but his passion still draws me to him. I doubt anyone will ever fill all my emptiness like Yves. Our time together wasn't blissful but it fulfilled me, I was whole at last. I had Yves and I had cooking. Together, they occupied my life enough that I didn't have to think of the past and the dark hole it left in me.

When Yves left me in Melbourne, it was as though he'd pulled the plug out of the drain and everything good and worthy trickled out. Returning home has thrust me back into the epicentre of my childhood pain. And now this aftershock of a pregnancy.

I can't understand how I conceived while being so careful. Yves liked to tease me about my paranoia. Once, when I said that being a parent was too big a responsibility, he responded, "But that's also a good excuse to play and enjoy yourself." I suppose that attitude might make him a good father.

Maybe that was why I never thought of my parents as good parents. They took being grown-ups seriously. There was no liveliness in our family, no humour. Expressing emotion with words or gestures was unheard of. You were to be silent, stoic, and mind your business. No wonder Yves appealed to me with his passionate speeches, fiery temperament, and the way his eyes gleamed when he talked about cooking.

If I were more like Yves, maybe I could express what I feel. Perhaps I wouldn't have lost him. Perhaps I wouldn't be in this mess alone.

The next time I go to the hospital, I find my father asleep. The pillow underneath his head seems about to swallow him. He looks fainter, as if he will just fade away one of these days, slowly disappear from his hospital bed.

I sit and watch him breathe, comforted by his light snoring, until I become drowsy.

"Nelida?"

I jerk awake on the chair. Through the vestiges of sleep, I realise he was calling for my mother. He's moaning and muttering, "I didn't mean for it to happen."

"It's me, Nina," I croak. I place my hand on his feverish forehead. "It's me, Father."

He stills. "Nina." His voice is a gravelly rasp. "I didn't think you would come."

"Of course I came," I say, feeling selfish for staying home the day before.

In the silence that follows, I begin to feel comfortable just sitting by his bed. He doesn't seem to mind me watching him because most of the time his eyes are closed. His throat gurgles and he coughs and chokes when he tries to speak.

I place my hand on his forearm and the sharp ridge of the bone brings tears to my eyes. The skin reminds me of baking paper out of the oven, rustling and dry.

He tries dislodging the phlegm in his throat by coughing. His eyes redden with the strain, and when his clammy hand slips on mine I'm surprised to learn he is still able to sweat.

I rise from the chair to press the help button above his bed but then his head falls back onto the pillow and he stills.

"Father?" I touch his cold cheek but his eyes remain closed. The absence of the cough is ominous. I try to see whether he is still breathing but I can't hear his breath over my quickened pulse and the blood rushing in my ears. "Father?" I shake him lightly, then more vigorously. "Dad!"

He inhales and then looks at me with his sunken, washed-out eyes. He shakes his head but when he opens his mouth, he makes no sound. His eyes flinch up and to his right. I fear he is having a seizure. The doctor has warned me they are common with his condition.

But then he stares at me. Until his eyes flit up again, in the same direction as before.

"Water? You want water?" When he nods, I feel useless and foolish for not having understood earlier. I grab the water pitcher and pour some into the thick glass. I hold it to his bluish lips and he wets them.

He rests his head on the pillow, pearls of fatigue gathering on his upper lip.

I imagine dealing with the elderly is a lot like caring for children; both are so dependent. This reminds me of my condition and I find it hard to breathe. I shake my head to get rid of the thought. It doesn't help. Before I can change my mind, I give in to the need to tell someone. "I'm pregnant."

For the first time today, he looks at me as if he sees me. I read the question forming in his eyes and to spare him the energy I say, "A co-worker."

I feel ashamed for making Yves sound so irrelevant and ordinary. I wish I could tell my father how much Yves means to me. How different he is from other men I've met. How he makes my heart race and my body warm up when he is near. But I can't because that is all mere memory now; a trace in the sand just above the low tideline.

"H-happy?" my father stammers.

My eyes fill with tears at my lying nod as I bite back the truth about thinking of getting rid of it, about feeling ill with fear, but also awed.

He mirrors my nod as if he knows the feeling.

It's disturbing how my baby and I are similar. My first thought after I grasped the reality of being pregnant was that I couldn't keep it. But when I think about how unwanted I felt as a girl, I wonder about my right to do the same to my unborn child.

Yet the image of responsible parents singing nursery rhymes and putting their lives on the backburner to care for their child clashes with the knowledge that I would resent stretch marks on my breasts, that I don't have the time, the energy, the will, or love to share. A child has never been part of my plans. I love my life in Melbourne, my friends, my dream job, the ease of being alone. Do I love all that too much?

"Love it," my father says, and startles me out of my thoughts. "Like it's yours." Fading again, he's talking nonsense, forgetting who I am, who he is. His eyes drift closed and then jerk open again. "Promise me."

"I promise," I say, wondering if I'm telling the truth.

Now that finding happiness with Yves is unlikely, I realise

how much I need him. Everything in my life is falling apart and I wish someone else would make the hard decisions. But I'm not even sure if Yves's presence would make things easier.

My phone rings and I yank the steering wheel, pulling the car into a lay-by. A cloud of dust rises from the parched gravel as I brake.

When I realise it's the hospital, I go cold. Has my father had another seizure?

The doctor's voice is familiar and professionally kind. "Your father just passed away, Miss Švagelj. It was peaceful and he wasn't in much pain. My deepest condolences."

It's not unexpected, yet it is.

The leather of the steering wheel feels warm on my forehead as I lean on it. I inhale, testing whether I still can, and I smell the scorched plastic of the dashboard and the dust motes in the hot, dry air. Mixed in is the smell of the hospital coffee and the lettuce and tomato sandwich on my breath.

Other than the vague sense that I should be experiencing profound grief, I don't feel anything. I'm inadequate; even when my father dies, I can't feel what I'm supposed to. What is wrong with me? I wonder. I comfort myself that I feel no sorrow because I've been expecting this. It has been a question of days, not weeks, and now it has happened.

When my eyes remain dry, I turn the key and create a fresh cloud of dust as I drive off.

Idleness is driving me crazy. Before the funeral, I've scrubbed our old kitchen clean and I need a new project to keep myself busy. But the weight of memories stops me from cleaning the rooms upstairs. I have yet to set foot in my old bedroom. The moment I walked through the front door weeks before and the memories oozed out of the walls, I decided to sleep on the couch in the spare room downstairs. Even there, I feel assailed by the house every night, by its immutability. It's as if it's telling me I'm indecisive, fickle, for having changed over the years while everything here stayed the same. My clothes, scattered around the dim, cobwebbed room, are out of place with their clean, fresh smell. But rather than tackling that mess, I focus on the living room next.

The room smells of flowers and smoke. Candles from the wake sit on the windowsill where someone has put them when they came for the coffin. I throw the candle stubs into a bin liner and open the window. I gather stray tea cups and a couple of crumpled tissues that have rolled under the couch.

The room slowly loses the unpleasant smell as I start cleaning out the cupboard. The top shelves with glass doors are filled with alcoholic beverages, which I pour down the drain. Below are three small drawers. One is filled with audio cassettes, there's an empty photo album in the middle one, and some documents in the third. I browse them and find my parents' wedding certificate and our old border passes. Underneath, there is another paper, folded in half. I feel the embossed stamp through the thick paper. I unfold it to find my birth certificate.

My name is written in neat cursive, but my father's name has been left blank. Where my mother's name should be, the wrong name is entered—it says my aunt Marija is my mother. I can't make sense of this. The mix-up with the names is ludicrous. And why keep a faulty document? Why didn't my parents throw it away?

I shake my head and drop the certificate back in the drawer.

Perplexed, I try to focus on sorting the rubbish. Of the things I have cleared out of the living room, I put everything that won't burn into two large cardboard boxes. The rest, I haul out into the garden.

Several times, the flames fizzle before they take to the damp heap. But once it gets going, the flames rise almost as high as the nearby apple tree. The garden glows from the fire and afternoon sun. The funeral yesterday was held at five in the afternoon to avoid the worst heat. The disapproving glances cast my way stung, but I couldn't conjure up tears by sheer will.

The cut-off jeans I wear now, a pair from grammar school I shortened with kitchen shears earlier, feel a smidgen too tight at the waist, and offer little protection from the intensity of the flames. The buoyancy of the heat gathers flecks of ash in the air and they stick to the suntan lotion on my skin, making me feel dirty.

Every now and then, I poke the fire with an iron rake I found in the shed, pushing the escaping items back into the inner circles of the inferno. The sun is mid-afternoon low when it vanishes behind a grey mass in the southwest. The rain begins soundlessly, snuffing out the last flames and drenching me. I welcome the refreshing coolness on my ashy skin. The drops falling on my cheeks—the salty and the sweet—are cleansing.

I am alone now. There is no one else, and I'm frightened. I jump when a gust of wind slams the back door shut.

When the storm passes, the last light of the day breaks through. The moist leaves of the apple tree smell of soft sweetness. A breeze rustles the leaves, the quenched landscape giving a contented sigh. The dust and staleness are washed away, the crust of the soil is softened, the grass refreshed. The smooth and mellow air mists over the valley like steam over a plate of stew.

I spoon coffee into the filter funnel and wait for the cafetière's satisfying hiss. I go into the living room and take my birth certificate from the drawer. I stare at it a long time as I drink coffee. What does it mean? My father and mother's names are absent from my birth certificate as they were absent from my childhood. I don't understand why. And with my father gone, I can't ask him.

I feel empty, languid, rid of a burden, but also broken. Sadness, relief, confusion, pity, an end, and a beginning are tangled into one. I'm unsure I'll know how to unravel myself. More tears will come now that they have started, and I'm ready to cry them. The ache is part of who I am. Perhaps hurt doesn't change your love but it changes the way you give it—hesitantly, cautiously.

TEN

I've kept the lights on the past two nights. The house has somehow felt emptier since my father's funeral.

I lie in bed for an hour but I can't sleep. I try reading at the kitchen table but my head droops to my chest. I startle awake when a knock rattles the door. I glance at the clock on the cupboard. Eleven o'clock is late for visitors.

I peer through the glass pane in the front door.

"I saw the light on," Silva says, when I unlock and open the door. A puddle glistens in the centre of the stone step where generations of feet have polished it into a shallow basin. "Are you all right?" she asks, shuffling her slippered feet.

Why is she here? At this late hour? "Your feet must be soaked," I say to avoid answering her question.

She glances down and her lips twitch as if she's about to smile, but she stops herself. "They make them better these days. One of the rare things. Leather soles."

I'm struck with the absurdity of our conversation, almost as if we are in a Woody Allen film, discussing slippers two days after my father's funeral. Life has a funny way of intruding on the seriousness of it all.

"The rain was good, though," Silva says, oblivious to my dark amusement.

"Want to come in for tea?" I've grown accustomed to

drinking tea since I returned. I think it's force of habit since my mother always had a pot on the range.

She follows me in but says, "It's too late for me, I'm afraid. A cup of tea at this hour, I might as well sleep on the chamber pot." My lips quirk in a grin. I wouldn't have thought it possible for the crabby old woman to make me smile. Unintentional on her part, I'm sure. "There are cracks two centimetres wide in the garden," she goes on. "I don't manage to water it, you see. A few spots, yes. But this was a godsend. The rain. I feared it would hail because of the heat."

From her rambling I know she is here for a reason that has nothing to do with the rain or improving my mood.

"Biscuit?" I baked them at five in the morning when I could no longer lie on the bumpy couch.

She pounces on the plate as if afraid I will take it away before she can take one. She drops onto one of the kitchen chairs.

As I pour tea for myself, I ponder how she's provided unexpected and much-needed comic relief. But that wasn't intentional. So why is she here? Last time, she shooed me out of her house when I asked her about my father. And at the funeral, she kept glancing at me, not curious or reserved like other people, but like she knew something I didn't.

"I've been watching you," she says, and I shudder at her ominous-sounding words. What does she mean? I stare at her, but she won't meet my eyes. "I think you should know the truth now you're expecting a child yourself. They're all gone now and it's not right that they kept silent. It's not my duty to tell you, but I might be gone soon, too, and there'll be no one else left." She stares at the crumbly biscuit in her hand. Her fingers tremble. "It's about Marija."

My hand pauses and I put the cup back down. How does she know I'm pregnant? And what has Marija got to do with anything?

"She had a child. That child was you." Her voice is firm, but she still doesn't look me in the eyes. "I guess these things happen often nowadays," she says, and glances at my belly. "At least we hear more often of them. Back then it was difficult."

The rushing in my ears is so loud I can't hear my own thoughts. I can't even form a proper question. "What?"

Silva raises her eyes, their steely grey colour glinting in the kitchen light. She hesitates before she repeats, "You were Marija's daughter."

Her skin has always been so yellowish I'm surprised to see her cheeks flush. "I don't understand," I say. "She was, well… I don't remember her ever being in a relationship." But her name was on my birth certificate. Was this the reason? Could it be true?

I press my hand to my stomach and collapse onto a chair. If Marija was my mother, then who was my father? Why wasn't I raised by her? Why did Nelida pretend to be my mother?

The sliver of almond on top of the biscuit crunches between Silva's false teeth.

My reflection in the fridge door finish is distorted, a hazy silhouette coming in and out of focus with the flickering light overhead. That's me: someone hazy who doesn't recognise herself, a ghost with an undefined, shifting outline. I don't have a home. I thought I knew my parents, but I was wrong. I'm pregnant with the child of a man with whom I have ended things twice.

Dizzy, I slide forwards and lower my head to my knees, breathing deeply, squeezing my eyes shut so I won't cry.

"Are you all right?" Silva asks. I hear the distant sound of her struggling to her feet. "I shouldn't have told you. I shouldn't have. Not with Franko… I thought, now that they're all gone and you're pregnant yourself, I thought you'd want to know." She steps towards me, but then she hesitates in the centre of the kitchen.

Without lifting my head, I say, "There's a bottle of water in the fridge. Could you pass it to me, please?"

Silva clucks. "You shouldn't. It'll ruin your stomach, cold drinks."

"Please."

Her shrivelled shadow slides across the wooden floor as she sways to the fridge. She pours the water into a glass, all the while admonishing me. "People die in the desert for drinking cold drinks."

"They don't drink cold drinks in the desert."

"How do you know? I didn't think you would drink it straight from the fridge, either." She makes it sound as though I'm planning to commit a hideous crime.

I straighten and reach for the glass. Silva clutches it to her stomach with both hands.

"Give it to me," I say, not bothering to hide my impatience with her.

The touch of the cold glass when she hands it to me returns some feeling to my numb body.

By retaining the water in my mouth and flushing it against the insides of my cheeks, I focus on the sharp, frigid feeling. I concentrate on the sensation until the last of the coolness evaporates and my mouth is filled with lukewarm saliva.

"Who's the father?" I slur the words. "Who's my father?"

"I don't know." She says it too fast. "When Marija realised she was with child, she broke down and told Nelida about the affair."

Silva lowers herself onto the chair next to me. She chokes on a breath as if the revelation pains her as much as it pains me.

Patting my hand, she shakes her head. "She was lucky she had your mother." Startled by her mistake, she jerks her head up like an alert turkey. "I meant… Well. They decided to keep it a secret. When her time was near, Marija moved in with your folks."

"I didn't know any of this," I say.

"I was a nurse in my day. They called me on a freezing January night. It was a full moon. Such children are always born at night, no?"

I'm tempted to ask what sort of children those would be, but Silva averts her eyes with embarrassment when she realises she's talking about me.

"I insisted Nelida held you first. It's only right for the baby to first get to know the person that will take care of her, no? Marija never forgave me for that. I was doing my best," she says, offended.

She's quiet for a moment, but it seems she's remembering the past because she then says, "'This child will never know she isn't mine,' she said, Nelida did."

She watches me. I can't hide the tear that breaks over the dam of my lashes and pride. "I thought she was my mother. But she lied to me."

Silva shrugs. "She had to. She was doing it for her

sister."

I'm about to protest, to tell her what I think about liars, but I realise I have no right to judge. I can't fathom what my mother and aunt went through. The impossible decisions they had to make, the heartbreak and pain, how they had to keep up the pretence for the sake of others at a time when they were at their weakest and most vulnerable. Could I really resent the lies? But I deserved to know.

After a moment, Silva says, "She couldn't have children, you know. She told me herself. They tried. There must have been something wrong with her because she couldn't conceive. Regardless of the circumstances, you were a blessing."

Her voice is like an echo. I'm too busy feeling sorry for myself at my family's betrayal to listen any longer. Perhaps a part of me has been aware of it all along, and that was the reason I wanted to leave here and why I could never settle.

How can our lives be so full of mysteries? The things I have believed my whole life, taken and turned upside down. It's not just that my house of cards has collapsed, it's like I'm only just realising it wasn't made of cards at all. My own skin no longer fits. I think of stretch marks and my hand goes to my belly of its own accord.

When I call the bistro, Miren answers. She sounds emotional even long distance. She's motherly towards all Philippe's employees. She dotes on Jeff and me, in particular. I'm not used to being taken care of and at times it suffocates me, but right now I wish she were here to comfort me.

Instead of an embrace at the news of my father's passing, I receive a flood of affectionate words, interspersed with bits of news from the bistro. I miss her with a physical pain in spite of the smile on my face.

"Ren, I'm pregnant," I say in the middle of her speech when I can't hold it back any longer. I wait. "Don't make me repeat it, please. I feel silly enough."

"Oh, no, don't. It's something to feel happy about, not silly."

"It wasn't planned."

"I can tell. It doesn't matter, Nina, love." She pauses, but only for a second. "Is it Yves's?"

I knew she wouldn't take long to cut to the chase. "Yes."

"And that's not a good thing?" There's a scratching, accompanied by the clatter of a knife on a stainless-steel surface. They are probably in the middle of mise en place in Melbourne as I stare through the musty curtains into the late summer garden.

"I don't even know whether to tell him," I say, more to myself than to her.

"You should, he has rights as the father."

I know that but I still wish someone would tell me it's my body, my baby, my decision, so it would ease my guilt about wanting to keep this to myself. Would it be such a crime if I kept the news from him? He's not part of my life any more. He would probably want this child less than I do.

I can't help but think about my father—my biological father. Did he know Marija was pregnant? Did he desert her before she told him and, alone as she was, she saw no other solution than to give the child to Nelida and Franko? Perhaps he knew and wanted her to get rid of it—get rid of me—and she refused.

As if Miren can sense my thoughts, she asks, "So, are you keeping it?"

I know she didn't even flinch as she asked. It has nothing to do with whether she condones abortion. She just poses the questions that need asking. She once told me how she had bought her fifteen-year-old son a pack of condoms when he was going on a date. The morning after, she asked him whether he had used them. He nearly died of mortification, but she considered it her duty.

"I don't know. There's something else." The silence on the line invites me to keep talking. "I've just found out I was adopted."

"God, you've had an eventful few weeks, haven't you?" Miren sounds as overwhelmed as I feel.

"I've never felt this miserable. Everything's gone to shit." I tell her about my parents.

"Whichever choice you make, it will be the right one for you," Miren says once I stop talking.

In any case, I can't go back and change my mind to see how things would have been if I'd taken a different path. I have one chance to make a choice. The way Marija made a choice. The way my mother did.

Yves arrives as I'm making stew. I open the door and see him standing there, and he says, "Hey", as if our last meeting months ago hadn't ended in a fight, as if he'd only been gone a little while. I gape at him. How come he is here? How does he know where I live? Why did he come? Why now?

His dear, familiar face doesn't fit into this place. The door handle feels real in my hand so I can't be imagining things. But it doesn't seem possible for him to be real.

"Philippe called yesterday morning," he says, his voice hoarse. His eyes drop to my belly and then return to my face.

"Philippe?" I haven't spoken to him in weeks. "Miren told him?"

Yves shrugs. "*Je sais pas.*" His scruffiness suggests he hasn't had the best of times since I last saw him.

Has Miren told Philippe it's Yves's? What did Philippe think? I'm not sure how much Philippe knows about Yves's and my relationship.

"I thought I could go with you to maternity classes," Yves says. The words come out in a rush, and the points of his ears turn pink. "If you'd like me to," he adds, as if it occurs to him I might not want him around.

I move aside so he can come in. He follows me down the hall as my heart hammers.

His teeth gnaw on his lip as I watch him, astounded that he is here. Him catching a flight the second Philippe tells him the news reveals more about how he feels about this child than words could. The thought warms my insides even though I don't delude myself that he's willing to patch things up between us.

"This is very traditional," he says, looking around the kitchen. "Very local colour."

My lips itch to smile at how uncomfortable he is. He isn't often out of his element. I've never seen his sure and practised fingers fumble like they do when he tries to push his phone into a pocket in his bag. The phone catches a couple of times before he succeeds. I wish I could put my arms around him but our past stands between us like a wall and I'm too exhausted to scale it.

"It's nice. Authentic," he adds, probably afraid I'll take his words as criticism.

He looks at a chair. "May I?" he asks. "It's been a long day and it's barely morning," he mutters, dropping onto it when I nod. It's ten in the morning, so he must have got up in the middle of the night to catch a plane, as his bloodshot eyes attest.

I step over to the worktop to get us drinks and calm my pounding heart. I scatter sugar everywhere as I prepare lemonade. When I saw him at the door, I thought for a second my mind must have conjured him out of sheer desperation. I wish things between us weren't so complicated. Even with the elation I felt when he walked in behind me, there's hurt mixed in as well. I ache at having him so near and not being able to say the things I want to because I'm not sure I can trust him. Or myself.

I place the glasses of lemonade on the table. His eyes rove around the room. His leg bounces under the table. I feel such tenderness towards him that everything in me quakes.

"I was making lunch—it'll be ready soon," I say, my voice brittle, and I sit on a chair opposite him.

"I don't think I'll be able to eat." His hand gestures to demonstrate the winding road that made him queasy.

I hide my smile. "It can wait."

Yves has the excuse of observing the unfamiliar room so he doesn't have to look at me. I, however, know every inch of the space and my staring at the wall would just be awkward.

The wind howls around the corners of the house. It has started early this year; it's barely September. I find it odd how perception alters solid spaces. The house feels bigger when cold, smaller when warm. Just like Yves seems less imposing with his jittery fingers and the tense lines around his mouth. Yet he's the same person I met three years ago. Or is he? I can hardly say I'm the same as I was then. I've been through so much, met new people, finished cookery school, buried my father, ended up being pregnant when I least expected it.

Above the wind, I hear the river. The water level has risen. Distracted, I wonder what defines it as the same river when it's forever changing. The only constant seems to be the riverbed and its location. But I refuse to believe I am defined by this place or that my home is limited to this village. I could never settle here. Could I? But what do I have in Melbourne that I don't have here? Could I raise my child so far from where I was raised? That Yves lives in Paris complicates things.

I stand to fill his glass from the pitcher, but he stops me, patting the chair next to him. I can't refuse without revealing how fragile and uncertain I am.

"You're keeping it, no?" he asks, his eyes on my waist, voice soft.

"Yes." The answer comes naturally although I can't say when I decided.

"I'm sorry about Melbourne."

"Me, too."

"You shouldn't be. You were right."

"Not about everything," I say.

The first day in cookery school when he walked down the hallway to welcome us at our lesson, I felt equal parts fascination and fear mingled with heady excitement. Things have changed since. Now it isn't fear of him, but of being without him.

"Let me get that lunch for you," he says, and stands. He stops my protesting with a quick gesture. "Let me, please." And somehow, I know that if I agree this will be a sign of welcoming him back into my life. His expression is earnest. The lines around his eyes are deeper, filled with more weariness than I have ever seen in them.

"*Merci*," I say.

His back turned to me, he says, "I'll book a room at the guest house in the village. Or do you know of a better place?"

With other people, that would imply I should invite them to stay at my house. With Yves, it means what he says. This knowledge of him has always given me a feeling of security and dependability. With his frankness, the ground beneath me won't shift or fall away; that I can rely on at least. And that is what I need now.

ELEVEN

In mid-October, more than a month after my father's funeral, I decide it's time to let the ghosts out into the open. I don't know if I'll stay in the house but even if I don't, I must clean out the rest of the rubbish to sell it. I hope, with more space and less clutter, it'll be easier to think, to decide, to plan.

There have been moments when I've been reluctant to throw away even the smallest thing, and then moments when I thought it would be satisfying to get rid of everything and fill the house with new things—my things. But Yves's presence gives me the much-needed balance.

The pile in the garden rises high with yellowed sheets, old newspapers, and boxes. The heap of rubbish by the front door has collapsed as it waits to be taken to the recycling centre.

I'm kneeling in front of the dresser in the master bedroom when I hear the crackling of the first flames outside. Straightening, I catch Yves wrestling a chair by its leg towards the burning mound. In the kitchen, his moves are like a dance. But he looks clumsy and awkward here. It makes him seem a different person; it shows his frustration, insecurity, rawness.

I sit back down and drag the contents of the dresser and both bedside tables onto the carpet. I find a thinning blonde wig, a lovely, if old-fashioned set of pants and bra still in its original package, old bills and postal orders, a folder with insurance policies, and an empty photo album. From under the rest of the debris, I dig out a hand-carved wooden box. I open it, and inside is a nosegay of dried flowers and a striped tie. I never saw my father wear a tie, not even for my mother's funeral. The only other occasion I can think of is their wedding.

The fabric feels cold and smooth under my fingers. The thought of how hopeful my parents must have been on their wedding day brings tears to my eyes. They must have had plans. What did they dream about? A large family? How they would renovate this house? Maybe move away?

They couldn't have imagined how things would turn out, how a baby would disrupt their marriage rather than make it happier and stronger. When did they realise things hadn't gone as planned? Did they just give up? From my memories, I can't say either of them tried hard to make it work. But then again, nothing in my memories hinted that they weren't my real parents either. I wish my father was still alive so I could ask him all the questions.

I place the box on top of the insurance folder on the bed. I sift through more of the clutter scattered on the floor with teary eyes. The chill penetrates through the carpet and into my bones.

When I join Yves in the garden, he is poking the fire. It now looks subdued and waning, but up close, it's still hot and invigorating. I extend my hands towards it to warm up after the cold bedroom.

"Okay?"

I nod and gesture to the streak of grey ashes across his forehead. He scowls. "I recycle my waste. I'm not used to burning the hell out of it." His voice is gruff compared to the delicate crackling of the fading fire. He looks up, bright flames reflected in his dark eyes, and shakes his head. "I didn't mean it like that."

"I know." And I do. I've experienced the frustration of being out of place enough times to know how he feels. "I'll take the rest of it to the recycling centre tomorrow."

Weeks ago, I lit the first fire in this same garden, but I felt different then. I'm no longer alone, and rather than dealing with the past, this time we're making space for the future.

For the first time in weeks, I'm enjoying myself as I cook dinner for Yves. I adapt my mother's recipe for roast beef. I heat up as I fall into the quick rhythm of preparation. I can't help but smile as the kitchen fills with the delicious smell of roasting meat.

We eat in silence, until Yves says, "This is excellent. Will you tell me how you season it?"

"Of course."

Yves stays at the kitchen table, and I put on a small pot to brew coffee.

"Want some?" I offer when the grounds settle in the pot.

"Please." I marvel at how even his voice sounds softer now than it did in Paris.

He sips his coffee standing by the kitchen cupboard and browses the postcards and knickknacks.

"I have to replace it," I say, gesturing to the cupboard. "The hinges are sagging and squeaky and the paint is peeling all over."

"I could fix it for you."

I glance at him over the rim of my mug. In exchange for what would he be willing to do it?

"Don't look at me like that," he says, clearly irritated.

"Like what?"

Yves rubs his face with his hand. "I'm not bartering for my child, Nina. I wouldn't offer if I didn't mean it. You know that. You know me." He places his hand on his chest. His gesture reminds me of the Valentine's Day back in Paris when we talked about knowing people. I long for those precious moments between us when things were straightforward.

"It's a strange situation, you have to admit," I say.

"I can see how tense you are. You keep thinking about what I'll do and say, and what you should do and say, and how things will go from here on, no?"

I pinch the bridge of my nose. It unnerves me how well he can read me, but it also feels good to have someone know the worst about me and not mind it. Like with everything when it comes to Yves, I am torn. "I don't know what we are," I say. "I don't know what to expect. I have to think of the future now." Had my mother—Nelida—felt so torn, too, raising her sister's child?

He presses his lips into a tight line. I'm taken aback that he is as affected by all this insecurity as I am. It shouldn't surprise me. Until now, his only responsibility has been his restaurant kitchen. Now he has a future to think of, a child.

Yves swipes the stack of old newspapers off the table. They explode in a rustling avalanche and scatter across the floor. He squeezes his eyes shut, head hanging low. He takes a few deep breaths, before he steps towards me. "We've found ourselves in a bit of a bind, yes," he says, his voice hoarse.

The loud pulse in my ears and the hollow in the pit of my stomach tell me it's far more than a mere bind, but I want us to solve this; if not for our sake, then for our child.

His skin is warm against mine when he presses his palm to the side of my neck.

"Whatever happens, happens, Nina. And if it doesn't, that's all right, too," he says, almost pleading. "You and I, we'll both be there for this child, no? We can be good parents regardless of everything else. As for us, we have to be grown up. Making a drama of it won't help. Let's take it one day at a time."

"What do you want?" I ask. The warmth of his hands brands me. This man can be passionate to the point of insanity, or not give a flying fuck about things. He mystifies me in a tempting way that forces me to care. I hate him a bit for it.

"I wish you'd accept me," he says. His hand drops from my neck to his side. "We were good together, before. There were problems, yes, and there will be problems, for sure. But life is only as complicated as you make it."

His words sound reasonable but for the life of me, I can't make them work for me. I drop onto a chair. This back and forth is exhausting. "It's just that you function on a different level to anyone else I know. To me, too."

He doesn't seem sure whether I mean it as a compliment or criticism.

"You still amaze me after all this time," I admit.

He shrugs. "We complement each other." He pulls a chair closer and sits next to me.

I decide we will have the chance to prove or disprove whether we complement each other some other time.

Now, I'm too afraid of what this might reveal, the cracks which could open up and swallow me.

"What are your plans?"

I've been asking myself the same question for weeks. "I don't know."

"How about Philippe's? Will you be returning to Melbourne?" He holds my hand, tracing lines on my palm. It occurs to me he might be afraid, too.

"I quit," I say.

He looks up. "He didn't tell me."

"I just decided." I stare at the cracked, cobwebbed ceiling. "Melbourne feels so far from here right now. I'm too confused to make plans." I sigh. I used to know who my family were. Even the resentment I harboured towards them was uncomplicated. However sad the past made me, I at least knew how I felt. But now… "I feel lost. I don't know who I am any more, who my parents were. And this baby… Worrying about a job feels so trivial. Like that's the least of my worries." The money I've saved over the years will last me a few more months but eventually I will have to decide what to do.

Yves puts his arm around my shoulders, pulling me to him, and presses a soft kiss to the top of my head. "Who your parents were doesn't change who you are," he says as if he can read my mind.

He has lost weight since Melbourne. His eyes seem deeper, cheekbones more pronounced.

"Doesn't it, though?" I turn to him. "My mother lied to me and I don't even know who my father was."

"But you're not them. You are talented and smart, you're passionate. You're beautiful. Beautiful in here." The pressure of his palm against my chest robs me of my breath. I cover his hand with my own in thanks.

The wall clock ticks away the silent minutes. I try to speak several times before I find the clarity to form my thoughts so he will understand. "It's not just that. I have my fa— adoptive father's name, a name that's not mine. I've lived abroad for a long time. After three months, I'm still more comfortable speaking English than my mother tongue. I don't feel at home here anymore. I don't feel at home anywhere. Melbourne was the closest to that. But now I'm here, it feels so far. I just want to get away from all this but I've run out of places to go to. Somewhere else is a state of mind I'm not capable of, it seems."

He looks upset. It seems as though he's trying to find words to comfort me but failing. His silent mouth joins warmly and softly with mine. Minutes later we end up on the living room couch. His soothing and gentle lovemaking unleashes my tears, and he brushes them away. As he presses me into the cushions, the sobs burst out of me. He murmurs *"je t'aime"* and it sounds like the most natural thing.

I now know the distance between us was partly my fault. I expected him to say things I was not willing to say back.

I have been confused most of my life—about myself, my place in this world, even my language. Just before Yves showed up in Melbourne, I had reached a point of contentment. I came to accept myself. But only days after arriving home, that person vanished, like a dissolving mirage. I was not Nina any longer, not the one I had known, anyhow. My name was Švagelj, and then it wasn't any more. The dips in my cheeks I thought I inherited from my mother are my aunt's legacy. Well, my real mother's, just not my mother's. And my mother tongue—what mother, what tongue?

I didn't know matters were so messed-up in my family, but I felt the distance even as a child, the silence that wedged itself between us. I longed to have someone to talk to, to laugh with. But I was forever alone, pushed to the edge of the family. Perhaps I tried to keep myself safe with detachment, far away, immersed in a different language. But loneliness translates into every language.

Yves's hotel room has stood empty for two weeks now as he spends his days and nights at my house. He sleeps on the couch in the living room. My dislike of the room has lessened since we made love there. But I still wonder if he feels any of the tension the room used to evoke in me as he lies there at night, alone.

I feel Yves's pull again, as I always do when he's near, but I'm not ready yet. I keep busy by cooking for him. I think he enjoys discovering new flavours as much as I enjoy introducing him to the dishes of my childhood. The food connects us but without the intimacy of a relationship I'm hesitant to rekindle.

"I don't understand where things went wrong," I say, as Yves puts away the lemon marmalade we made that morning. The jars glisten with sweet juices like the setting sun captured in a glass as he carries them to the pantry. He cleaned it out the week before, finishing off my meagre attempt at throwing away stale food and years-old jams. We've restocked it with fresh preserves and compotes, just in time for winter as November is around the corner.

"Why do you think anything went wrong?" he asks.

"Silva said my mother had craved a baby, but she was

never there for me. I know I wasn't hers, but it's not like that was my fault." My words remind me of what my father said in the hospital. "You were my daughter. She wouldn't let me forget that." If she felt as though I was their daughter, why was she so cold to me? Why remind my father I was theirs but then behave as though I was an intruder?

Yves glues the labels onto the last batch of jars, his hands working with a precision reminiscent of surgical theatres not a country kitchen.

"Maybe she loved you in her own way?"

"She ignored me most of the time. Same with my father. It feels wrong calling them my parents when they never behaved like proper parents."

"You're obsessing."

I resent that he can't be bothered to understand as I struggle to comprehend where I came from, who I am, who my family were.

"Sometimes the burdens are too much, Nina. Look at how you're reacting to the news about your parents. Put yourself in your adoptive mother's shoes." He puts his hands on my shoulders and their weight anchors me. "Maybe she wanted to love you, but couldn't. In some people, the instinct to protect themselves is too strong. They avoid any love that could hurt them. So they keep themselves distracted by gambling, making preserves, constructing La Tour Eiffel out of matchsticks, moving as far as they can, or just staying close and being detached."

He has summed up my life and the people in it in one sentence. My father and mother, Marija, me, even himself. Making preserves. For whom? Does he subscribe to the same future as me? Are we planning for those preserves to be eaten by the same people? Or will they be thrown out the same way as the ones my mother made years before and were left forgotten on the pantry shelves?

Or maybe his words are an apology, the only way he knows how to say he is trying his best. He is here and this means something. He is the only one still sticking by my side, even though I must be driving him mad.

He leaves the house in a huff to go for a walk after he's finished with the preserves. Perhaps he feels he's not enough to ground me and it's eating away at him. I feel sorry for him but I can't help it.

When I see the neglected graves, I realise I came unprepared. Silva urged me, before my father's funeral, to come clean the graves and bring flowers, for "What will people think if you don't?" I didn't want to upset her by telling her how little I cared what others thought but I didn't tidy the graves either.

I find a couple of paper tissues in my purse. Kneeling, I wipe the grime from my mother's headstone. All of a sudden it seems much longer since her death, as though I lost her a decade ago. The moss in the corners of the stone adds to the impression. But some of my memories of her are still vivid.

I recall her ignoring Marija as she perched on the edge of her chair while my mother and I ate plum dumplings, the kitchen silent except for water dripping into the sink from time to time, the sound like a full stop to an unspoken sentence. I cannot understand my mother's coldness to Marija. They were sisters. And my mother could be warm and kind. The way she laughed until tears ran down her cheeks as we shelled peas, her patience as she taught me to cook and let me try the most complicated recipes even if I failed. We laughed over a soufflé with its top sunk like the crater of a volcano. I shared happy moments with her.

The letter L in my mother's name on the tombstone has fallen off. In the oncoming dusk, I have trouble finding it between the needle-like leaves of the winter heather. The coldness of the metal letter when I find it at last seeps into my core. I huddle deeper into my jacket to banish the chill.

My father, too, was different when we were alone from how he was when others were present. He would let me help him in the garden. He taught me how to split firewood with a small axe when I was eight or nine. I wonder if that was his small revenge for my mother allowing me a knife to peel potatoes. Was it his way of saying, "See, I trust my daughter with a sharp object, too"?

"You were my daughter. She wouldn't let me forget that," my father said. There was something in the way he said it that nagged. A feeling I couldn't quite grasp when I remembered his tone, the look in his eyes.

I see them facing off across the kitchen table as if I were back in our kitchen, a clueless six-year-old. "Are you trying to tell me how to raise my daughter?" my mother says.

The memories don't add up. Something in my childhood was awry, misaligned. Something still is. I can't trust my memories and what they're telling me. The grave feeling in my stomach spreads and grows, and I grasp onto the only fact I have: I'm Marija's daughter and my father is un—

My mother couldn't have children, Silva said. How did

she know? Unless she had proof that my father could have them. "You were my daughter." My mother reproached him. Was that why she hated him? Because he was my father. My biological father. Is it possible? Did she hate her sister for having an affair with her husband? It couldn't be.

I look over the graves to the mound of soil at the edge of the cemetery. The wreath on top has withered; the wooden cross has listed as the soil has dried up and dipped.

A headache blooms to life behind my eyes as I'm flooded with recollections, so distant but as acute as if they were all happening again, right now: Marija reading stories to me in secret as if she is initiating me into a secret society. Marija saying, "Your mum would be upset if she knew I gave you the doll when it's not even your birthday." My father and Marija sitting at the kitchen table as far apart as possible, speaking rarely, about mundane things, their tone carefully indifferent. My mother smiling when she says Marija has never learned to cook. Her taking the polka-dot dress from Marija so I couldn't have it. My father saying, "Love it like it's yours" when I tell him I'm pregnant in the hospital. I thought it was his medicated mind talking nonsense, but what if he was remembering the past?

Each one of them—my mother, my father, Marija—featured in separate memories in my mind, as if they purposely isolated themselves after having been too entangled. As if it was less taxing for them to be detached and angry than to deal with each other.

What if my mother's struggling to love me wasn't because I wasn't hers but because I was theirs, the result of an illicit affair and the constant reminder of their betrayal? Did Nelida resent her sister for being my real mother? Maybe Marija, in turn, resented Nelida for getting to raise me as her own daughter.

The more I think about it, the more sense it makes. It would explain why Marija was so afraid to show me affection when my mother was near; why my father could build sandcastles with me but withdrew into himself in the presence of my mother; why Marija gave me gifts in secret and hugged me so desperately when no one watched. Perhaps even why she succumbed to her demons. My family had fallen apart long before I realised it, before I was even born.

I thought finding out that Marija was my mother was the strangest thing that could happen to me. I was wrong. An affair between Marija and my father is even more bizarre. And I'm more and more convinced it must be the truth behind all the hatred. The only way to confirm it is to wheedle the truth out of Silva. She kept telling me snippets of the past, instructing me to come clean the tombstones, asking questions. Has she been giving me clues?

I drop my car keys on my way to the car and then fumble with them as I try to start it. I manage on my fourth attempt. I realise I'm holding my breath at how the puzzle pieces now seem to be falling into place. I've been seeing all the patterns and parallels for a while but I only now understand them.

I regret I didn't try harder, as an adult, to forgive my parents. So many hours spent sitting silently by my father's sickbed, wasted. I could have asked him why— why didn't they love me? Why did they push me away?

Insist he tell me the truth. Admit to him I felt betrayed and hurt by their indifference. But even if I'd acted differently, nothing would have changed the past or prepared me for the truth.

I drive around the bend and the moonlight reflects like quicksilver on the river's surface. Through my tears, the two solitary houses ahead appear blurry. Pale light seeps through Silva's kitchen window. I park the car in front of my house. Crossing the road fast, I don't give myself the time to reconsider what I plan to do.

In a decade or two, my child will start asking questions. I could lie. I could avoid answering. I'm good at avoidance. But I've also experienced being lied to and the hurt it caused me. I need to know the truth.

I knock on Silva's door and enter without waiting for her to invite me in. She comes into the hall, switching on the light. When she sees me, dishevelled and hands covered in soil, her face falls.

I open my mouth, but she turns and goes back into the kitchen. The act angers me and I hurry after her. I find her slumped in a chair. Her wispy hair is sticking out in all directions; her face looks drawn, different. She sighs and I see she's removed her dentures.

"Tell me the truth, Silva, please," I say because I can't be harsh with this withered shadow of a woman. "Tell me about my father."

Her chin trembles and she shakes her head. At last, she lisps, "You already know or you wouldn't be asking."

I bend to her level. "So it's true that Franko was my father?" My voice wobbles, but not as much as my heart. "He and Marija had an affair?"

Her mouth opens and closes in a silent stutter until she

finally nods.

"Did Nelida know?" She's silent for so long I don't think she will answer.

She sniffles and then wipes her nose on her sleeve. She looks up and her eyes meet mine. Then she says, "She found out after you were born." Her gaze becomes distant. "They were lucky they had Nelida."

"What do you mean?"

Silva looks at me as if I am stupid. "She swallowed her heartache and raised you like you were hers, didn't she?"

I never felt as though I was hers, but I don't tell Silva that. I can barely admit it to myself.

I crouch there for another minute but she doesn't speak or look at me again. She doesn't react as I straighten. I leave her slouched like that in her kitchen. On my way out, I turn the hallway light off.

My head spins as I make my way back to my house. I stumble into the front door but then it opens and I fall into Yves's arms.

"*Doucement*," he says. For a moment, he just holds me and it feels right to be here.

"Tea?" he offers when he accompanies me to the ratty old couch in the living room. He wants to leave, but I hold onto his arm and the couch sags under him as he sits. I lean into him.

"This thing has to go," I say.

"What?"

"The couch." I look around the dim room and think of a number of ways it could be improved. Perhaps the unpleasant memories could be pushed to the background if I created new, better ones. "I need a new bed, too. And bookcases. You could help me order new windows before winter."

"It's getting late for that. You should wait till spring," he suggests, his tone soothing as if he knows every thought that went through my mind moments before, of my heart stumbling as I try to cope with the new knowledge and decide whether to tell him yet or not. "It can wait," he repeats. "All the work will wait. Don't stress yourself over it. It'll all still be here once you feel stronger. I'll be here."

"I'm fine." I say it without thinking but when I consider it, I don't feel as awful as I would have expected after such a discovery. I'm rattled, yes, but at least now I know. Perhaps with time, I could come to accept it.

"Good. That's good. I didn't think it would take you this long, though. I thought you'd sooner see what I see." He sounds weary and relieved.

His words surprise me. "What do you see?"

He takes a long while to respond. "You're focusing too much on the past. Sure, it's who you are. Or part of it. But it's where you're going that's the most pressing question, *n'est-ce pas?*"

"I know who my father was," I blurt.

He doesn't say anything, but his eyes widen a fraction.

"My father, who I thought was my adoptive father—it was he who had an affair with my aunt."

"You were their child?"

I nod.

"I see." Yves pauses, then adds, "Yes, it makes sense when you think about it."

We sit in silence after that. The fire in the kitchen range roars so I can hear it through the open door and the clock ticks evenly, unperturbed by everything it has seen throughout the years. I envy it its aloofness.

Yves's caress on my hair feels awkward but his relaxed expression suggests he isn't averse to practising the gesture. He's stopped using his nickname for me. It belonged to a different, less significant period of our lives.

"Do you think I'm self-absorbed? Self-centred?" I ask, thinking of how consumed I've been with memories for the past few weeks. I haven't noticed much of anything outside my obsession with unearthing the truth.

After a moment, he laughs to himself. Another moment passes before he says, "You'd need a centre to be self-centred. But you are all over the place, grasping at this and that, trying to find yourself. You're trying too hard." He holds me tighter, keeping me together, maybe afraid I'll fall apart.

"Yes, but all of it is me, even the trying too hard part. This is me. The depressed mother I didn't know about until weeks ago, the burning need to run, but also the hope of finding my place. The worrying about how long you'll stay and if we'll agree on a name. This is me, Yves."

"I know. Now you need to accept it and let it go."

"Won't I be letting go of myself?" I know his words are wise; I have come to understand his reasoning over the past months, or maybe I'd started to see it even earlier, little by little, from the very beginning of our relationship.

"Don't take yourself so seriously," he says.

I make a promise to myself to heed his advice.

At night, I lie alone and as the old bed in the master bedroom creaks and my ribs are poked by the bedsprings and kicked by the baby, I cry. But it's a cleansing cry, more out of relief than any real grief. It no longer hurts, not in a sharp, jarring way. Maybe I have found my place after all.

Maybe it's in me. A spot I hadn't realised was there because it got buried under a heap of lies, misconceptions, and guilty consciences.

I think of the house and how the air in it is thick with memories. I can't part with it but I also can't live in it as it is. Decluttering it was just the first step, now it's time for me to come to terms with the past before the house can become a proper home.

Two days later, I'm scheduled for an ultrasound. I'm relieved when it shows a healthy boy.

I help Yves clear the blankets and pillow from the living room couch later that day. I don't want to waste any more time being afraid of all the things that might go wrong between us. Things will always go wrong and we'll deal with it. Later that night in my bed, he tells me he had been hoping for a daughter, but all that matters is that the baby is healthy.

Philippe calls to tell me that after a few weeks of searching he has found a replacement for me. I don't feel a part of Philippe's any longer; I haven't for a while. I accept the news with relief. Maybe I will return to Melbourne someday. The months I spent there were some of the most joyous in my life. It was the happiest home I've known, as far as geographical places go.

It is also where I started to think differently about cooking. It has always been my hiding place. I escaped to cooking when I was confused, torn, heartbroken. But then I started rediscovering my mother's old recipes to find something I could cook for Walt. I regret that he came to the bistro too late, after I left. I regret that it was too late to cook for my father. The only time I cooked for him was the two weeks when I was home after my mother died. Two weeks of simple pastas and stews, long before I even imagined I would one day become a chef.

I often browse my mother's old cookbook to find dishes I think Yves will enjoy. The memories sometimes make it difficult but I've accepted the past so I can move on. Cooking is no longer something I can lose myself in; it's where I have found myself. I seem to have a roundabout way of doing things. I've travelled to the other side of the world to find home. I had to get lost before I looked up and realised, "Oh, so this is where I am. This is who I am."

Yves is afraid I will regret getting rid of the old furniture from my childhood room, but I want the nursery to fit this child, this life. The changes in the rest of the house are becoming more apparent with each piece of old furniture I replace with a new one and with each wall I repaint. The new soul in the old house is slowly emerging. I realise I'll never brush aside the past but this is as fresh a start as I can have. It's a process, a collage of emotions and questions, of visits to the graveyard to meditate, to accept what's happened, to plan what's to come. Yves is generous with his support and I'm learning that I don't have to be alone in this if I so choose.

EPILOGUE

There isn't a shred of doubt in my mind, when I open my own restaurant, that I should serve traditional Slovenian dishes. But I also let all the other places where I've lived inspire me.

Years ago, I would have been willing to do sixteen-hour workdays in the hope of one day receiving a Michelin star. That's all gone now. I'd rather spend my time running through the rustling summer grasses with Teo. That gives me more pleasure and calm than I ever imagined possible during my uneasy pregnancy.

Still, some evenings, on escorting the last patrons out and closing *Ninočka* for the day, I have a rush of that driven feeling again. I still dream of success, only its definition has changed. I don't aspire to reach the stars; my wishes are closer to the earth. Satisfied patrons and happy employees, room for creativity and innovation, the chance to grow at my pace. I've found my place, and now I need to mould it to who I am. The menu changes as fluidly as I do, with the seasons, with experiences.

I have come to terms with the fact I am who I think I am, and that DNA strands, language, and a birth certificate only determine my identity as much as I allow.

Teo kicks the ball across the garden to me. He waits for me to return it, watching me with a guileless face and

Yves's dark eyes. Who does he see when he looks at me?

"Time for bed, little man," I call after him, as he runs to catch the runaway ball.

He shakes his head.

"Oh yes."

It's one of the longest days of the year. The sunset is the colour of peaches. It turns Teo's hair into a reddish halo.

We went to the graveyard earlier. He placed a bunch of flowers on each of my parents' graves. When he asked who those people were, I was honest. I didn't want to hide the truth from him. Even though he doesn't understand now, he will one day. The truth is convoluted but being honest with him helps me be honest with myself. The moment I admitted to myself I was angry, sad, and bitter because of what had happened, the emotions were easier to bear and my parents' decisions easier to accept and even understand.

Sometimes, I invite Silva to lunch at my house. Every time I see her she seems smaller, as if she will slowly disintegrate rather than die. And she always compares my food to my mother's cooking. Undoubtedly, her aim is to disparage my modern twists on the old recipes, but I don't mind. She's my last link to my parents and I'm grateful for that connection.

Teo protests now when I call him in, but when I pick him up, he leans his tired head on my shoulder. Summer days are long and tiring for him, but I love that they give us so much time to spend together outside.

I often work the lunch shift so I can spend the afternoons with Teo after he returns from nursery school. The hours of play are intense and drain me of energy but fill me with a deep happiness I have never experienced before. Still, the quiet once he goes to bed is welcome. I enjoy nothing more than sipping a glass of wine and relaxing with a book or just absorbing the serenity.

Being a single parent means a lot of togetherness with my son, but also a great deal of loneliness. It's in those moments I think of how my relationship with Yves has changed, of how we kept coming together and breaking apart until we finally ended it two years ago. He comes to spend a month or two with us every now and again, and he has moved to a more spacious, child-friendly apartment for when we visit him in Paris. Every time I see him with Teo, my choices are vindicated. I used to think that of all the men I've been involved with, Yves was the worst choice. Now I know there has never been any choice, it was how it was supposed to be. I might meet someone else one day, but there will always be Yves. He is that sort of a man. Or maybe I'm that sort of a woman. Sometimes, when we see each other after a long time, hope overwhelms us and we end up together for a day or two of what-could-bes. Invariably, we part. But there are no regrets. Never any regrets.

Acknowledgements

Several people were instrumental in the creation of this novel. I would like to express my deepest gratitude to Jasmine Donahaye who was my dream supervisor during my doctoral studies. She always asked just the right questions to make me dig deeper and think harder until *The Landscape of Loneliness* and the entire research project was far better than it could ever have been without her expert and kind guidance. Jasmine, you made my doctoral journey enjoyable from start to finish. Thank you. *Diolch o galon.*

The foundation for this novel was laid decades ago when I first started learning English as a clueless but curious eleven-year-old. Nanda Zega, my first English teacher, opened the doors and windows into a wide new world for me when she introduced me to the English language and culture. Without her endless patience and kindness, I wouldn't be where I am today. *Iz srca hvala.*

A big thank you also to Susan Buchanan for proofreading the manuscript when it was still in the form of a PhD dissertation. Thank you to my friends Elodie Katan and Audrey Cresta who patiently answered my questions about the French language and culture. I owe you one. Also, to all the lovely people at Cinnamon Press, particularly Jan for helping me make this happen with her generosity and understanding, Rowan for editing, and Adam for the design. Thank you, Jessica Bell for the gorgeous cover.

A heartfelt thank you to my parents and grandparents who are nothing like the family in this book and who have always supported me in whatever I chose to do. Thank you also to my sister who read one of the drafts. She said the story was morose so I knew I was on the right track.

And to my boys, thank you for being who you are.

Milton Keynes UK
Ingram Content Group UK Ltd.
UKHW022341080324
438952UK00004B/22